# Made of Rust and Glass

## Midwest Literary Fiction, Volume I

# Made of Rust and Glass

**Edited by Curtis A. Deeter, Shannon Holleran, Leah McNaughton Lederman, Jonie McIntire, and Andrew Reising**



**Published by:**
Of Rust and Glass
607 River Road
Maumee, OH 43537

**Typesetting:** Curtis A. Deeter

**Cover Art:** Kelly Brown

ISBN: 978-1-7367728-7-4

*To anyone who has ever identified as a
Midwesterner. These are your stories, your voices.*

# About the Cover Artist

Kelly Brown is a mixed media artist originally from Toledo, Ohio. She graduated with a BFA majoring in Illustration from the Columbus College of Art & Design in 1996. Since 2002, she has run her small business, Art by Kelly, which for 12 years focused on mural painting and specialty faux finishes, but now is centered on window painting and fine art. Since 2014, she has participated in many art gallery shows, art fairs, and local art festivals. She is also the owner of Mini Miscellaneous and creates mixed media miniatures. She does social media marketing & design for Carpets by Otto.

Our cover image, a mixed media work on wood panel titled "The Message," was created using real vintage stamps, real vintage ledger paper, collage with printed tissue paper, an image transfer of the bird illustration, and acrylic paint. A photography filter was added last to enhance the sepia tones. The themes of the painting are travel, handwritten letters, and nostalgia for home. For those included in this anthology, the Midwest is home, no matter how far they may have traveled.

# The Rancher

## by Dan Denton

*Dan Denton works as a chief union steward at the Toledo Jeep Plant, and he's a writer and podcast host. He is the author of four chapbooks of poetry, and his writing has appeared in dozens of zines, newspapers, and anthologies. His debut novel $100-A-Week Motel is out now on Punk Hostage Press and has thus far received rave reviews.*

A man stood, flattened hand over worn brow, eyes squinting, looking over a snow-covered field. The sun, just newborn in the morning sky, was screaming sun rays like babies do, but they were plastic sun rays in the February morning. The plastic rays skittered off snow diamonds sending the white-hot light of snow blindness racing across the prairie.

A golden retriever pup just shy of her first birthday was playing freeze tag with an imaginary friend, zigging, zagging, jumping into and out of snow drifts.

The old rancher smiled, the lines in his forehead relaxing as the small lines around his eyes tightened. He let his hand down from blocking the sun, sipped coffee from the mug in his other hand.

"C'mon girl," he hollered, "you're gonna be a snow dog you stay out any longer." And the rancher laughed as the retriever pup raced to the back door of the old single-story ranch house.

The rancher and the dog went in through a sliding glass door, to a warm kitchen, where the man got a Milk Bone dog biscuit out of an open red box and gave it to the dog. Patting her on the head after and saying the things you say to an almost one-year-old puppy, in the voice you use when you say the things to an almost one-year-old puppy.

He set his coffee cup down on the counter, opened a big refrigerator, looked inside for 11 empty seconds, before closing it again. A page from a superhero coloring book fell from a magnet on the fridge to the floor, and the man bent and picked it up and tucked it back under the magnet. He thought of his three-year-old grandson, the Crayola artist that had colored and torn out the page. The grandson was off in Denver with the rancher's youngest son, and the son's wife. The picture from the coloring book was of Iron Man, and red and yellow crayon scribbles were almost inside all the lines.

The rancher went to a closet-sized bathroom off the kitchen. He stood and relieved himself, then washed his hands. He looked at the mirror, drying his tough hands on a soft, worn hand towel. The face in the mirror looked like a face that had stood 60 years squinting at high-definition prairie suns.

The man got a biscuit out of the refrigerator, and put some jelly on it, and sat at a kitchen counter barstool, and ate the biscuit cold, between sips of black coffee.

The golden retriever pup got up, and sat by the man, and he gave the pup the last bite of the cold, crumbling biscuit.

He switched on a small kitchen counter television, flipped through three channels to find the morning news. A new president was promising compassionate relief measures, more on that after the weather. More snow was expected.

There was a news story from the city about a young man shooting three kids, ages 1, 3, and 5. The newscaster reported with a mechanical voice that police speculated the violence stemmed from a domestic dispute.

"The hell is wrong with this world?" the rancher asked an empty kitchen. The retriever pup looked up like she was wondering, too.

The rancher changed the channel on the small kitchen counter television to ESPN. Former athletes were talking hyper chatter about the super bowl the night before.

He got up and opened the refrigerator again, looked inside for 11 empty seconds. Turned and asked the stovetop clock what time it was, and when the stovetop clock answered 8am, the man shrugged a response and got a beer out of the fridge. He twisted off the cap and went and sat back down on the kitchen counter barstool and took two sips of morning comfort from the bottle.

There was a book on the counter, and the rancher slid it over. He liked to read, here at the counter, in the evening after chores were done. He'd sit here on this barstool and read, while the evening news recounted the day's horror stories and his wife of 40 years stood over a stove and oven working to turn ingredients into suppers that roadside cafes have never quite learned to recreate.

The book was called *The selected poems of Wendell Berry*, and the rancher had read the book a dozen times already, but it was a good book with good poems, and good poems are good poems forever no matter how many times you read them, and the rancher was reading them again because it was winter, and winter was hard on the open prairies, and Wendell Berry poems made him feel good when he read them, so he was reading them again as a way to warm his resolve so as he might again survive another harsh prairie winter.

The man turned the book open to a crumpled napkin bookmark and read a Wendell Berry poem about farms coming to life in the spring, and the phone rang, and the man went to answer it.

"Hullo," he answered.

It was the nurse from the Intensive Care Unit at the big hospital in the city. "She's still the same as yesterday. No change." The nurse said.

She was talking about the rancher's wife. She was five days on a ventilator, sick with Covid, and the rancher hadn't went a single day without seeing her, without kissing her good morning and good night, until now, and it had been a week since he'd dropped her off.

"Want me to hold the phone up to her again?" the nurse asked.

The rancher said he did, and he waited there listening while the nurse moved the phone over near his wife's ear so she could hear.

The coffee pot beeped its shut-off beep. The refrigerator motor kicked on, starting up its hourly hum-mantra. The kitchen sink dripped once, and the golden retriever pup lifted up her head from her nap.

The rancher said, "Hey Thelma, my biscuits ain't as good as yours, and you know I make the coffee too strong. Me and Sadie Dog are ok, and ole Wendell Berry says if we just hang on long enough this old ranch will come back to life again in the spring. We just gotta hang on, Thelma, you hear?"

And the rancher stood there, phone to ear in a suddenly noisy kitchen, that was, somehow, still empty.

# The Girl and the ATM Dispute

by Dan Denton

A factory working man sat in his Jeep waiting behind three cars to use the ATM machine at the bank branch up the road from his house. He'd just gotten off work, a 10 hour shift down on the assembly line at the local auto plant, and he needed to stop by the weed guy's house to buy his weekly ounce of wind-down-from-the-factory comfort.

B.B. King's Bluesville, Channel 74 on satellite radio, played a harmonica solo from some old-time blues man that capitalism had long forgotten. The factory man drummed an unconscious drum beat on the Jeep's steering wheel, as his thoughts drifted to his evening's chores. After he saw the weed man, he needed to pick up coffee, milk, and cigarettes from the corner store, and he thought maybe he'd buy a couple of lottery tickets. In the middle of a no-luck winter stretch, something was bound to give eventually, he thought.

A Kia sedan fished out a transaction receipt and moved on to whatever business a Kia driver would have after visiting a money machine.

The factory man inched the Jeep forward. A green Honda sat with a white hand leaping in and out of its window, the hand playing capitalist music notes on a tired and out of tune looking money machine. An old maroon Dodge minivan sat farting black exhaust from a rusted-out muffler in front of the Jeep, and the factory man sat thinking lottery dreams while satellite beams transformed into a long, sad guitar solo, this time from a new young guy that capitalism still hadn't discovered.

The green Honda with the dancing white hand finished its business and moved on, and the raggedy, turning to rust Dodge minivan burped two large black clouds of desperation and heaved forward to the out of tune money machine.

The factory man inched the Jeep forward, almost as an afterthought, turning the volume up six clicks of the volume button behind the right-hand side of the steering wheel on the Jeep. A John Lee Hooker song was on B.B. King's Bluesville, and ole John Lee was wailing sad notes in 1080p high definition. The factory man was shopping for beach houses in south California on lottery dream money. John Lee Hooker cut through like a rusty steak knife, dragging the man back to the now, singing about having no money for the rent.

The factory man remembered cold nights from a past life, nights spent wide awake, wandering through war zone alleys, chasing salvation via crack pipe, and drowning in cheap wine.

He shivered, looking up. A commotion ahead. A 30-ish woman with hair dyed blonde three months ago in a trailer park kitchen was hanging out of the driver's side window of that minivan with a stuttering engine and an exhaust in need of Pepto Bismol. She had a bright pink wife beater tank top on and a pink thong just peeking out above gray sweatpants racing to catch up as the woman hung there banging on the money machine with both fists.

"Screw you, you no good f*^$#!!"

"Give me my stinking money you mother-falooting frankenstein."

The woman wailed as she blasted the machine with a full-on class 2 felony assault.

*Bam.*

*Bam.*

*Bam.*

She punched the machine crying and screaming and the factory man sat in his new Jeep, John Lee Hooker hitting third gear in full on, can-barely-keep-my-head-above-this-drowning-ocean blues. The factory man's eyes wide open, wondering how much longer it would be before he could get his money and go get his ounce of feel-good weed.

He pushed the button to lower the window and leaned his head out, as fat snowflakes began to fall on tiny parachutes drifting from an already graying sky.

"Hey lady, how much you need?"

"Forget you," she yelled back, hitting the machine two more times before turning her head to look to see who was yelling behind her.

She hung nearly half out the driver's window of the rusty minivan, so that she was nearly upside down when she smiled at the man in the new Jeep behind her.

"You got $40?" she asked.

# Even Amateur Cooks Learn How to Pair

by Jonie McIntire

*Jonie McIntire, author of* Semidomesticated *(Red Flag Poetry, 2021),* Beyond the Sidewalk *(Nightballet Press, 2017) and* Not All Who Are Lost Wander *(Finishing Line Press, 2016), hosts a monthly reading series called* Uncloistered Poetry *from Toledo, Ohio. Learn about her at https://www.joniemcintire.net.*

All I had to say was *shredded pork*
*with homemade hot sauce for dinner*
and he put down his beer,

stopped his computer game,

even ignored the blips of his iPhone
to walk over to the kitchen
with a kiss for me.

He didn't even flinch at the once-hated
greens shredded and hiding
in the sliders or the dreaded
sweet potato baked into the bun.
Didn't mention how his arms and back
hurt from mowing the lawn earlier,
from line trimming and struggling

with weeds I refuse to touch.

Just bit in, closed his eyes and whispered
*delicious – all together, delicious.*

# Three Poems
## by Robert Beveridge

*Robert Beveridge (he/him) makes noise (xterminal.bandcamp. com) and writes poetry in Akron, OH. Recent/upcoming appearances in Panoply, Torch the Veil, and Otoroshi, among others.*

## Screen Saver

The wind picks up, ruffles
thc flag across the street.
It is red, with one white cross
at its center. Beneath it,
the green of bushes overtaken
by the red and black of ants
who have never worked together before.
The berries may be poisonous to men,
but other species thrive here.
They scatter at the first
few drops of rain, seek shelter
in somersaults.

# No Obvious Signs of the Sheep Remain in the Vehicle

the devil stole the savior's hand and put him in the meadow
the devil stole the savior's hand and put him in the meadow
the bomb is in the cherry tree, the trigger in the well
the devil stole the savior's hand and put him in the meadow

the banners sing the drone police with red eyes into blue
the children handle acid while they seek the evening's food
the banners sing the drone police with red eyes into blue
the banners sing the drone police with red eyes into blue

the cotton weaves, the fire burns, the morning falls to night
the cotton weaves, the fire burns, the morning falls to night
the cotton weaves, the fire burns, the morning falls to night
the sign calls out its desperate need in city's distant slum

the elder calls the ritual, the devil bows his head
the grave is dug, the prayers are said, the savior turns to dust
the grave is dug, the prayers are said, the savior turns to dust
the grave is dug, the prayers are said, the savior turns to dust

# Trailers for Films that can Never be Made

A biopic of your two years
in an Israeli prison that culminates
in the great escape where you
exited the train stage left
on the way to Bucharest.

We asked for the funds
to produce the 24 hour long
green screen movie but were
told no one would watch
a green screen for 24 hours.

The exposé on the underbelly
of random acts of kindness day
you tried to produce with the cash
you'd embezzled from the Ghanaian
mafia continues apace even
though the distributor's warehouse
went up in a blaze of gasoline,
roman candles, and a piquant
pomegranate/chayote slurry
three nights ago.

Marilyn Chambers was in talks
to play the lead role in a revival
of *Titus Andronicus* until we
discovered she'd been gone a decade.

And Jason is dead. Get over it.

# Dinner for Six on County Road C

## by Paul Lewellan

*Paul Lewellan retired after fifty years of teaching in Midwestern secondary schools and private colleges. Now he lives and gardens in Davenport, Iowa, with his wife Pamela, his Shi Tzu Mannie, and her ginger tabby Sunny. He has recently published fiction in* Intangible *Literary Magazine,* Coastal Shelf, Rhodora *Magazine, and* Talon Review. *When he isn't writing, he stocks Little Free Libraries with his favorite books.*

"The cows are in the corn," Jill said, out of breath. "I'm so sorry."

"I beg your pardon?" John Lloyd's caller I.D. read *Jillian Babbitt*—his supper date in 45 minutes.

"It's Jill. The cows are in the corn. They got out while we were at 4-H."

"So…you're running late?"

"I need the daylight, John," she said in exasperation. "We'll be lucky to round them up by tomorrow."

He set down his shaving kit. "Want a rain check?"

"A rain check?"

"You can't go to dinner tonight but some other time…once the cows are in."

"Sure—I mean, yes. I'd like that."

That satisfied him. "Need help?"

Jill laughed at the suggestion he could. "Do you know a lot about cows and corn?"

"I don't know shit about either."

"The corn is high, and when you step into it, you can't see or hear anything until you're on top of a cow."

"I have a drone and two teenaged daughters who would recognize a bovine on sight."

"You're sure? It's hot and dirty work."

"The girls will be eager to help." He waited.

"Tell them to wear shoes and socks, not sandals. Boots would be even better. Long-sleeved shirts, jeans to cover their legs, and a cap for their hair."

John changed into his third best pair of Levis, a worn plaid shirt, Keen hikers, and cotton socks. In the family room, his eldest daughter groaned. "You're wearing that on your date?"

"Yes Lizzy, I am."

"She will be impressed."

"Judge for yourself; you're about to meet her. The cows are in the corn."

Lizzy put down the August issue of *Cosmo*. "Are you being allegorical?"

"I am not. Jill's cows have escaped. I volunteered you to help retrieve them."

She gave him a withering look. "And why would we do that?"

"Because then I will return your iPhones, laptops, and tablets; reinstate your Internet privileges, and unground you."

His younger daughter Kay, seated at the other end of the couch, whistled softly. "She must be some sexy farmer." She was going to be a high school sophomore in the fall. Kay held up her copy of *People* magazine. "I can see the headline. 'Single Parent Sacrifices Daughters in Daring Divorcée Cow Capture'."

"*Exactly*. You game?"

A week earlier, the girls told John they were going to a youth group lock-in at St. Stephen's Lutheran Church: a night of board games, Bible trivia, and fellowship. He signed their permission forms. Later, when he called the pastor offering to bring tacos after the hymn sing, he learned there was no youth group lock-in. It took him five phone calls to find the party, another to get the kegger busted.

Lizzy looked at Kay and then back to John. "We're in."

It took twenty minutes to drive from their suburban home to the farmstead north of Maysville on County Road C. In the front yard an old metal bedframe lay buried up to its sides with a flower bed in full bloom. At the fuel tank an older boy—tall, baby-faced, muscular—pumped gas into a mud-covered John Deere Gator. The younger boy was reed thin, sitting on an ancient red Kawasaki Mule. Both ATVs had been manufactured before the boys were born.

"Someone's been shopping at Walmart," Lizzy commented.

"My date tonight," John said, shutting off his SUV, "works this farm while raising two boys. She's done it single-handed for a decade. If you plan to insult her lifestyle or their wardrobes, stay in the Murano."

Jill stepped out onto the porch. She'd pulled her brown ponytail through the back of her John Deere cap. She wore a black tank top and loose chambray shirt. Her faded jeans were tied at the ankles of her prosthetic legs, the titanium rods disappearing into thick-soled work boots.

"Ever been on a farm?" she asked the girls when they approached.

"Third grade field trip," Kay confessed. "I didn't save my notes."

"Not a problem." Jill motioned for them to follow her. "Here's the situation: The ears of corn are tasty this time of year, very tempting to cows. The stalks are so tall you won't see anything until you run into a cow. Spook it, there'll be nothing but broken corn stalks as she escapes."

John put his drone in flight.

Jill's younger son Preston asked, "What's that?" His hair was curly brown like his mother's.

"That's my radio-controlled quadcopter with a live video feed."

Jill's fourteen-year-old son Barlow approached. He was 6'3" and wrestled heavyweight on the Varsity team in the winter.

"Stop distracting my sons." She pointed, "The cows are in the North Forty."

When the drone reached the field, John put the viewer on panorama and motioned for Barlow to look. "There are four cows in one group and two in another."

"We'll divide up," Jill suggested. "Barlow can take Kay and Preston on the Gator and go after the bigger group. Lizzy rides with me." She handed John a walkie talkie. "If we get these bovines back in the barn, we might salvage this date." She winked.

The path to the field was rough and there was no way to talk over the roar of the Mule. Finally, Jill shut off the machine and listened. Nothing.

"Do you get out much?" Lizzy asked.

"What do you mean?"

"I mean, you had a date tonight with Dad, but the cows got out. The date was a big deal for him. He's been acting weird since Tuesday but wouldn't admit to anything until last night when he told us." She made eye contact. "Was it like that for you?"

"Not really."

"Why is that?"

"I get offers." Before Lizzy could respond, Jill got off the ATV. "Let's have a look." She led the way, walking the rows.

"How long since your divorce?"

"Mid-December, eight years ago."

"What happened?"

"That's none of your business."

"You're dating my dad."

"Not yet."

"Oh, I get it. That's what tonight was to be about."

Jill paused. "I messed up."

"You didn't let the cows out deliberately. Cut yourself some slack."

They walked to the next row listening for cows.

"Thanks for coming with him."

"Dad bribed us. If we helped tonight, we'd be ungrounded."

"You were grounded?"

"We told him—no, that's not true—*I* told him we were going to a church sleepover. My sister said she wouldn't rat me out if I took her with me. I knew it was bad the minute I saw all the senior boys circling her, trying to get her drunk. I shouldn't have put her in that spot. And when I did, I should have had the guts to get her out of it."

"Have you told your father any of this?"

"God, no."

"You should. File it under lessons learned."

The walkie talkie squawked. "Two cows are three rows to the north of you."

"Roger that."

"Want a suggestion, Jill?"

"Sure."

"Send Lizzy down the row to herd them to the end where you grab them. She wouldn't know what to do if she caught a cow."

"And whose fault it that?" Jill's accusatory tone took him back. Then she added, "Just messing with you, John. Good idea. We'll take it from here."

Two hours later, as darkness fell, the last cow settled into the barn. "Well, that's that," Kay proclaimed. Her clothes were filthy, and her cap was askew, but she was beaming.

"Hardly. The cows have to be milked." Barlow turned to his mother. "And we're starving."

"You and Preston take care of the cows while I clean up and John fixes supper."

"You're going to milk them yourself?" Kay asked.

"No," the younger boy explained, "machines do that. Nobody milks cows by hand anymore, haven't for decades."

"I'd like to see that."

"Come on, then." Barlow looked over to Lizzy.

"I'll pass," she told him.

Jill wiped her hands on her jeans. "I'm going to take a shower so at least one of us isn't gross." She winked at Lizzy before turning to John. "You can fix supper."

"What am I fixing?"

She pulled out a pen and wrote on John's palm. "That's the number for the Casey's General Store. We'll need at least three large pizzas if you hope to get a slice. Say they're for me, you'll get extra sauce. Brandon and Preston are carnivores. Think Bacon Cheeseburger or a Meat Galore. I like veggies, especially mushrooms. You know what the girls will eat. Wings and breadsticks are optional. I've got plenty of soda." She smiled. "I'll be beautiful by the time you get back."

"Mission already accomplished."

Jill pointed at him. "Don't mess with me, mister. I have Kay for a hostage."

"I guess I'm fixing supper," John told Lizzie.

"Give me that." She grabbed his phone and steamed to the car. "I'll call it in. You drive."

When she finished the call, she waited. John avoided eye contact and kept silent. Finally she asked, "Is this woman another of your projects, or was this supposed to be a real date until the cows escaped?"

"You mean, did I know about her missing legs when I asked her out?"

"Something like that."

"Jill came for legal advice. Later, over coffee, I learned she was born without fibulae. At fourteen-months, doctors amputated her legs below the knees."

"Dad…" Her voice was tired. This wouldn't be his first pity date.

"Lizzy, she played lacrosse in high school. She runs the farm. She told me the missing limbs *weren't a big deal.* That's when I asked her for a date." John focused on the road. "And even with shit on her boots, she's an attractive woman."

"That's what I needed to hear."

The boys set the table, then lounged on the porch with Kay. When Jill joined them, she'd changed into a pale blue sundress and replaced her transtibial prostheses with her blades.

John and Lizzy returned with four pizzas, cheese bread sticks with marinara sauce, and a double order of buffalo wings. "Supper is served."

Over pizza, the group recapped their cow adventures. Kay explained the milking machines to her father. The boys talked about their 4-H project.

"They're Nigerian Dwarfs," Brandon explained. "I started the herd three years ago. Preston started working with me last year."

"Pigmy goats are less than two feet tall but can product two pounds of milk a day." Preston asked Kay, "Want to see them?"

"Are they cute?"

"You wouldn't believe how sweet they are."

"Maybe after supper…." She glanced over at Brandon. "I know nothing about farming," she said coyly.

"I was raised in the city; I learned 4-H along with the boys," Jill admitted to the girls. "Think twice before you marry a farmer."

Lizzy looked up from her plate of wings. "No danger."

"Life is unpredictable. Marrying a farmer was the last thing on my mind when I started my clinical in physical therapy." She glanced at Brandon. "But my first day working in rehab I met Dale, this giant man, freak of nature, who grew up in Iowa, played rugby with reckless abandon, and fretted over soybean futures."

"You were smitten?"

"More like…curious. I kept Dale at arms-length until I graduated, but his parents wore me down. They owned the farm and shared their love of it with me when I came to visit. It's a Century farm. Now there's no way I'd rather live."

"And what about my dad?" Kay asked. "How did you meet him?"

"My farmers coop hired him to lobby the state legislature. We want to sell unpasteurized milk."

"Don't you have to kill the bacteria?"

Brandon jumped into the conversation. "Heating damages the milk proteins and the enzymes. And people with gastrointestinal issues can't drink pasteurized milk."

"Farmers can sell to individuals now," Jill added, "but our dairy group wants to sell milk at farm stands and through cow-sharing agreements."

"Cow sharing?" When Lizzy elbowed her to shut up, Kay turned on her sister. "I want to know. This is interesting."

"Individuals pay a fee for boarding and milking the cows they own. They get quality and consistent raw milk. We're guaranteed an income." Jill set down a half-eaten slice of cheeseburger pizza. "But I suspect that the unpasteurized agenda wasn't why your father asked me to coffee, or why he bribed you to chase cows."

Lizzy smirked. "His motives *are* transparent."

After supper Jill told the kids she'd take care of the leftovers. "Brandon, maybe the girls would like to play a video game?"

"Call of Duty: Black Ops 4," Preston called out.

"I will kick your butt," Kay warned him. "You don't stand a chance."

"What about you, Lizzy?" Brandon asked. "Four can play in split screen mode."

"Why don't you three start without her," Jill suggested. "She can join you in a minute."

Kay followed Preston into the house, calling back to Brandon, "I will destroy you." He hurried to catch up.

Lizzy shook her head. "That poor sap."

"I think Brandon can hold his own with Kay," Jill told her, "after he gets over being awestruck." She combined the remaining pizza slices into one box.

Lizzy picked up paper plates and disposable silverware. "He's a smart kid, but not my type."

"What is your type?"

"Strictly university. Brandon's fourteen. I'm a senior. What does he think is going to happen?"

"Fourteen-year-old males are incapable of rational thought in the presence of a female like you."

"What do you mean 'like me'?"

"Intelligent, independent, strong-willed, unafraid. He thinks you're gorgeous, of course," Jill added, "but it's the other stuff that makes you interesting." She picked up the pizza boxes. "I'll put these away, then I have a proposition."

She returned with a large ice-filled wash tub stuffed with bottles of Fat Tire. She set it on the floor between their chairs, opened one for John, then opened another beer and handed it to Lizzy.

His eyes widened. "My daughter's too young to drink."

"Oh, John…" Both of the women laughed as Jill grabbed one for herself. "When I wasn't much older than her, I worked as a slammer girl."

"What's that?" Lizzie wanted to know.

"I wore a uniform: cutoffs, a halter top, and a holster with 7Up on one side and tequila on the other. My high-heeled boots covered my legs past my knees. Most men never realized my legs were missing. I kept shot glasses on a bandolier, and I would troll the bar approaching males—sometimes females, with the right vibe—and I'd say, "How about a shot?""

"That's it?" Lizzy looked over to her father, who shrugged, and then back to Jill. "'How about a shot?'"

"In that outfit," John clarified, "she wouldn't need to say much more."

"Tips were great."

"How old were you?"

"Twenty-one, if anyone asked."

"That took guts!"

"At that time in my life, I had limited choices."

Lizzy waited for further explanation, but none came. "When I saw your prosthetic legs, I thought, 'Crap, how does that work—'"

"Missing limbs aren't a problem." Jill leaned towards her. "Tammy Duckworth lost her legs in Iraq, got elected to the Senate, and had a baby. A double amputee climbed Everest. People run marathons in their prosthetics. I have issues with trust and commitment, but I've never had a confidence problem."

Jill finished her beer. "You mentioned you're job hunting…. How about working for me?"

"Doing what?"

"I have sweet corn almost ready to pick. I'll sell what I can at the farmers market and then take the rest, blanche it, cut it off the cob, and freeze it."

"That sounds like a lot of work."

"It's easier with two of us. And you'll be an asset at the market stand. You could start this weekend. If we have any energy left, on Sunday we could cold pack tomatoes."

"You really think I can do this?"

"It'll be nice to have another woman around, Lizzy. Plus I know you won't take crap from the boys. And after the sweet corn is in, I have painting, repairs, and cleaning that I never can get to. It's just minimum wage—"

"Deal," Lizzy said, much to her father's surprise.


With taunts and disorder, the three youngsters appeared at the door. "Kay demolished us," Preston moaned.

"Utterly crushed," Brandon added.

Kay beamed. "We're going to see the goats. Want to come, Liz?"

"Sure." The four of them spilled off the porch into the barnyard and made their way to the shed.

Once alone, John took a breath. "Remind me again about the goats."

"Dairy goats."

"Of course. I don't know jack shit about goats."

"Or about me, for that matter."

"I know that even without legs you're the most eligible woman in the tri-county area."

"And I know my way around a bailer."

John stopped laughing when he realized she wasn't joking. "There's a steep learning curve, isn't there? Dating a farmer?"

"You're doing all right. Most men would have helped with the cows expecting some reward. Few would stay for a family supper." She moved her chair closer. "Probably not the evening you'd envisioned—"

"Best date I've had in three years."

Jill pursed her lips. "That's how long since Elizabeth passed?"

"Yup."

"Your first date since then?"

"Basically. I've gone out a couple times…"

"So…?" Jill stopped. "Why now? Why me?"

"My daughters told me I needed to get out more."

"And you always listen to your daughters?"

"Never. Well, almost never. Sometimes Kay makes sense."

"Don't underestimate Lizzy. She's strong-willed. Bright. Eager to escape to college at the same time worried you'll be hopeless without her."

John rolled the cold bottle over his forehead. "You got all that from her, and you had time to herd cattle? I'm impressed."

"I told her I could relate to her struggles."

"Really?"

"I am totally clueless. My childhood was nothing like hers." Jill shook her head. "She hides the pain well."

"The pain?"

"The loss of her mother." She touched his arm. "You folded your tents when your wife died." John started to protest. "It took you three years to ask a woman out for coffee. And then you asked the most incompatible female you could find: a legless farmer with two teenaged boys— and she's a *client?*"

"Technically, the Scott County Cow-Sharing Coop is my client." He stopped. "Let me try again." He took a breath. "My daughters' relationship with their mother was complicated. They lost her twice. First, five years ago when I came home from a hearing in Des Moines and found them alone in the house. My wife told the girls she needed to pick up a couple items at the grocery store but didn't come back."

"Sounds like my husband."

"Eighteen months later, she returned with a small suitcase and a terminal cancer diagnosis. We reconciled before she died, but her passing left me angry and abandoned. I'd sworn off women, until you walked into the office."

"Kismet?"

"Admiration."

"Lust?"

"Oh, yes, definitely that."

"My marriage ended remarkably like yours, minus the cancer." She sighed and picked up another beer. "Mid-December, eight years ago, the day we finished the fall tillage, my ex suggested we 'celebrate a successful harvest.' I woke up the next morning, groggy. He'd put something in my wine. He made the boys pancakes, told them not to wake me, grabbed the $2500 in our cash box, and drove off in his F350. The boys were three and six. Police found the truck in long-term parking at the airport along with a note that explained he wasn't cut out to be a farmer." She huffed. "He grew up on a farm, earned an Ag degree from Iowa State, and at thirty-six, had never worked another job."

"Go figure."

"What could I do? The farm doesn't take care of itself. Neither do boys. It took two months to track him down. Nine months later we divorced."

"But you got the farm? How did that work? This is a joint property state."

"He didn't own it, his parents did. When he abandoned the family, they deeded the farm to the boys, to be held in a trust until they completed college and came back to run it. I administer the trust and draw a salary as the farm manager. I get a percentage of the annual profits, assuming the farm makes a profit."

"Dad!" Kay shouted as she approached the porch. "You've got to see these goats." Her older sister trailed behind, then the boys.

"It's late…," John demurred.

"Why don't you come out for dinner on Sunday? You can see the goats then," Jill suggested. "If you're free?" She didn't wait for him to answer. "Lizzy will already be here helping with the canning. She and I will make spaghetti. You and Kay can toss a salad. The boys can set the table."

"What about my rain check?"

"Let's see how dinner goes, but I suspect we'll be seeing a lot of each other."

John detected a smile on Lizzy's face. "That's why I was thinking, too."

# Even at the Surface

## by Tessa A. Adams

*"I postpone death by living, by suffering, by error, by risking, by giving, by losing."—Anaïs Nin*

Genevieve got up from the soft gray sofa and shivered. She looked out the window at her large backyard, covered in a flawless blanket of white. The chill from outside found a way to invade her space. It gave her a sort of unbalancing. She pulled her robe tighter, relishing the soft fabric on her bare skin. Genevieve walked into her bathroom, leaned over the porcelain, claw-footed tub, and began to run a bath. She smiled, welcoming the steam rising up from the scalding water. The feel of it on her skin softened her in her hard places no longer his. Restored.

She carefully grabbed two glass oil bottles from the shelf and added four drops of lavender and four of peppermint into the tub. Even. She put her head closer to the water, closing her eyes, letting the scents have their way with her. She opened her eyes when she heard the tapping of her dog's toenails on the tile. Mama, her Pomeranian, looked noiselessly at her from the bathroom's doorway. Turning her head as if to question Genevieve, she sat in statuesque, fur perfectly groomed. No matter what task Genevieve performed, Mama always took it so seriously. It was the kind of attention that could go to a person's head if that person was left alone for long enough.

The day he died, they had screamed at each other for hours. They waded through the usual topics: his infidelity, her inability to give him what he needed, his incessant work schedule. She surprised herself with feeling. Having been numb for so long, she welcomed the fire. Misery, rage, lust, depression. They were all related. Cousins at a family reunion. The feelings frolicked inside her and came over her all at once. A sort of drowning.

The kettle protested, reminding her the water for tea was done. After making herself a cup of chamomile, she pushed shuffle on her playlist and smiled when she heard Mazzy Star's smoky voice sing "Fade Into You." Genevieve turned up the volume. She returned to the bathtub at the perfect time and turned the water off. Setting her tea mug on her cup holder, she loosened the tie around her robe and let it fall to the floor. Her skin, hungry for warmth, bumped up in response to the warm water as she submerged each leg.

"A pension for violence." That's what the police officer told her the next morning. They had been watching him for a while. How could strangers know what he was capable of, but she—his wife of ten years—never knew him at all? Ten years, treading water. Each year, slowly slipping under. She flipped through his case folder that night at the station, reading the violent ways he solved business problems. It was for the best that he was through. What was it they called that? An eye for an eye?

Genevieve lowered her entire body into the water, her knees, head, and top of her breasts the only parts of her catching air. She lay her long, bruised neck against the back of the tub, put her body all of the way under, taking her head with her, scalding while cleansing. She enjoyed the sound of the world while submerged. The echoey distortion of Mazzy's voice washed over her pushing her lids closed.

When Genevieve was young and just learning the kind of damage a man could do to a woman, she watched her dad and mom like underwater dancers. Beer brought it out in her father. And music. Fierce eyes, veins in his neck, mother cowered. Her headphones took away the sound, and she could see them interact as if it were a silent film.

"Cry, cry for you…" In the nineties, life outside of her home was so quiet. She was convinced Mazzy would never make it in today's loud world. Genevieve used to seek noise in club corners, car backseats, and Friday night jam sessions. Looking for her own kind of choreography. Maybe the noise she now fought to smother was a penance. A sort of universe balancing. The yin to her yang. After all, Genevieve craved balance, smoothness, her own sort of scale.

The police went along with her story without looking too hard into it. Falling down the stairs had killed so many men before him; it made perfect sense that intoxication allowed him to dive down the two flights of stairs outside of his office plunging into an eternity. "He was alone, working late. I'm sorry, Mrs. Sperry." She surprised herself at how easy it was to feign sadness, and she pulled her collar tighter around her neck, a sea of bruises. She remembered the view of her leaving his office, getting into her car, and driving home. How stupid he thought her to be.

Although she had no office to call her own, she worked her whole life, too, for the feeling of even. From the outside, their coupling was perfect, balanced. For

Genevieve, it was more of an accounting. Scale: 126 pounds, no more, no less. Skin: Smooth, tanned, oiled, even. Hair: Strict bun, no fly aways, everything in its place. Him, a man to match her woman. Even.

Genevieve, still submerged, thought about staying that way. An eye for an eye. She the payment for his death. A wash. She faded, in and out like a light house light, beckoning, deciding, and questioning again. She heard Mama's cries in waves, saw the little paws on the tub's surface, and floated gently to the top of the water, even with its surface.

# Back In The USA Daycare

by Gerry Sarnat

*Gerard Sarnat MD's won San Francisco Poetry's Contest, Poetry in Arts First Place Award/Dorfman Prizes. Nominated for Pushcarts/Best of Net Awards, Gerry's published in* Hong Kong Review, Tokyo Journal, Buddhist Review, Gargoyle, Main Street Rag, New Delta Review, Arkansas Review, Hamilton-Stone Review, New Haven Institute, Texas Review, Vonnegut Journal, Brooklyn Review, SF *Magazine*, LA Review, NY Times *plus by Harvard, Stanford, Dartmouth, Penn, Chicago, Columbia presses. He's authored collections* Homeless Chronicles, Disputes, 17s, Melting Ice King.

Fruit just allowed to
ripen on the vine's sweeter.
Does that mean toddlers
sequestered, home with parents,
perhaps are better off now?

# Towers Leaning

## by Mitch James

*Mitch is a Professor of Composition and Literature at Lakeland Community College in Kirtland, OH and is the Managing Editor at Great Lakes Review. You can find Mitch's latest fiction at Flash Fiction Magazine and Scissors and Spackle, poetry at Peauxdunque Review and Southern Florida Poetry Journal, and scholarship at Journal of Creative Writing Studies. Find more about his work at mitchjamesauthor.com, and follow his Twitter @mrjames5527 and Facebook @perhupsous.*

June wasn't sure what bled down her mural or who did it. She peered across the dark yard at the four-way stop, a single streetlight above, then back at her art, a deconstructed Big Mac and fan of fries spread in pieces at its base. A pickle stuck to the mural, a streak of special sauce forming a crust beside it. Then there was the orange goo. Whatever it was bled down the installation, sticky and crystallizing in the cold air.

She had constructed the installation using weather-treated lumber, then built an awning over the top and two walls on the side. It created a telescoping affect which enhanced the 3-D design of the mural, an abstract version of the soul constructed of paper mache and rare wood she'd stolen from a logging site in Nigeria while there for the Peace Corp. She weatherized the installation by framing it in bricks she stole in the dark of night from the jobsite where they were tearing down the iconic eighteenth street bridge, a poplar place for lynching in the twentieth century and suicide by jumping in the twenty-first. To learn to lay the brick, she took a course in masonry at the local community college, a course that ate up all the money from her part-time jobs, forcing her and Barret to live off just Barret's income the entire semester.

That's why he had said no.

No, they could not add another fuse to the breaker box. No, they could not run a weather-proof extension cord from the house to flood lights that'd light the mural. No, they could not just let the meter spin its ass off all night, their money pouring down the drain.

She could clean the pickle and special sauce, but that orange goo, calcifying, stripping the finish from the wood, somehow gnawing like acid through the paper, it was too much. The mural was ruined.

"It's ruined?" Barret asked when she told him. "What's ruined? What's 'it?'"

The TV lit the side of his face in the dim room. "My piece," she said, hooking the neck of four empty bottles between her fingers and carrying them to the kitchen.

"What do you mean ruined?" he asked from the other room.

"I mean ruined, Barrett. As in not fixable."

"There's different kinds of ruined," he debated. "Do you mean like it's cracked or like it's in ashes?"

June pinched the hard bottle necks between her thin fingers until the sharp pain turned to hot wires of heat, then released them with a rattle into the recycling bin.

"Somebody threw shit all over it."

Barret dropped the leg rest of the recliner and sat up. "What kind of shit?"

"I don't know! Some kind shit, Barrett! Does it matter? The mural's ruined. But you know what, it wouldn't be if it were lit up, if we could see the yard and when people are sneaking around to vandalize our property."

"Jesus. Not that again," Barret volleyed, standing. "If you want to buy a lot of shit for the house, you have to work more. It's a simple equation."

"I have two jobs. And where are you going?"

"Two part-time jobs," he corrected. "You need a real job if you want to buy things we don't need. And I'm getting my boots. The party is in forty-five minutes."

"Fuck. The party. Are we really doing that? You're already drunk."

"I'm not drunk," Barrett said, returning with his boots. "You're just picking at me because you're mad about the mural." He stopped and looked at her. "I'm sorry about your piece. I really am. I know how much your work means to you." He studied her face, waiting for the acceptance of his contrition before sitting.

She knew he understood how important the work was to her. He was an artist too, once. A metalsmith. Jewelry mostly. She thumbed the promise ring he'd made her while in the MFA program where they met. He fashioned such beautiful work from the earth. She worried. Loving a man that no longer created seemed harder somehow.

"Such assholes," June said, her shoulders slumping.

Barret kissed the top of her head and sat to put on the boots. "Besides, lights don't make bad people good. Bad people do bad things, no matter what you do."

June's anger was waning to exhaustion. She didn't have the heart to fight with him about the lights that were never there and about the damage that was.

June changed in the bedroom and tried to put her hair into a cute bun, but it looked more like a top knot made from the hair of a toddler's bathtub Barbie. There was a little rouge, a little eyeliner, and two swipes of lipstick. She wasn't good at matching it all on any given day so felt content that she'd even made an attempt for a party she cared so little to attend she'd forgotten all about it. Though Barrett hadn't made a sound, she found him pacing the living room, eyes darting from the game to the clock.

"Ready?" he said.

June nodded.

"We got to get some rum on the way," Barrett said, flipping off the television. "What?" he asked, seeing June's face. "As a gift for Marquise and Brianna for throwing the party."

"So we're not in a rush then?"

"I never said we were."

"You said we needed to go. You sprinted across the house in the middle of a discussion to get your boots."

"Sprinted?"

"Let's just go."

"We'll be fashionably late," Barrett joked.

"Let's be fashionably not there."

"Great, June. Wonderful. Merry Christmas, everyone!" Barret yelled.

"No. I'll get the keys," June snapped. "You're not driving."

Barrett turned and walked out the front door, leaving it open behind him.


"Fashionably late," June snipped as they inched past the full driveway, people in Christmas sweaters, drinks, and small paper plates in the bellies of the bright windows.

"Better to park in the street anyway," Barrett said. "We won't have to fight our way out of that mess."

"No, we just have to walk two blocks in the snow."

"It's not like you're wearing heels," Barrett said, staring across the dark cab at her. "Besides, the sidewalks are clear," he finished.

June parked the car, and they made their way to the party in silence. She could hear the music and voices grappling in various pitches of base and treble on their way up the porch steps. The windows were cracked. June could already feel the suffocating effects of the people and their warm breath and body heat like a lethargic pulse inside the house. She felt bilious.

People cheered as they entered, Bing Crosby's joy buried below their noise. Barrett smiled and held out his arms. In crowds, he became boyish, so personable, the joker, like nothing ever phased him. It's something that drew her to him, the idea that no matter what the world brought, no matter what she did, he would handle it optimistically, opportunistically, make the world's pain meaningful. As people joked about their tardiness, Barrett dropped his head sheepishly, grinning and blushing as he ran one hand through his frazzled hair. He's like a giant child, June thought. The two of them hadn't been out together in a long while, both always working, their spare time spent in domestication, shopping, cooking, cleaning. She didn't remember the last time she saw him aglow with that childlike luster. It made her want to hug him. Then, she thought of the mural and the extension cord and lights and the background sounds of sports and the clank of empty beer bottles in her hands. Where was this boy all the other days? She wasn't violent but could slap him right then.

There were hugs and handshakes, compliments on hair and clothes. There was the difficulty of balancing small plates between pinched fingers while mincing through the too-full rooms of turning torsos and jutting elbows, keeping a safe distance between others and drinks. As suspected, the room was full of heat and, but for the outburst of the occasional guffaw, was a steady buzz of chatter with a muslin cloth of Christmas music draped like breath behind it.

When the tops of the holiday dips filmed over and the corners of sliced cheeses hardened, Brianna and Marquise brought out a half a dozen boxes of Jenga. They said they'd been buying them at secondhand shops or ordering them on eBay since last Christmas, when they decided they wanted to throw a holiday party and needed a fun game.

Barrett, across the room from June, set his drink on a windowsill and clapped. "Yes!" he exclaimed. His face was cherubic with heat and alcohol, his hair thick and wild. A few others laughed and clapped. This made Marquise and Brianna smile.

"Alright," Marquise said, "Pair up by couple. All y'all single folk, take a seat!" People laughed.

June looked at Barrett across the room. Grinning, he grabbed his drink, then licked his hand where liquor had splashed over the rim of the glass.

"You ready?" he asked, kissing June on the neck, his breath an iron mill of heat and rust.

"I've never been very good at this."

"How is that possible?" he questioned, too loudly. "Everything you build is a masterpiece. Just look at—" he burped, his mouth closed. "Just look at your mural," he finished, after a cough.

Marquise and Brianna cleared a table with chips, dips, and a charcuterie board and replaced it with six identical Jenga towers, all painted to look like Christmas trees. Somebody awed as they stacked their blocks, and others followed.

The six couples stood around the table, the singles to the side, drinks in their hands. There was a prize for the winning couple, Brianna explained, pulling a rectangular box with a bow from a closet and leaning it against a wall.

The couples took turns, easily using pointer fingers to inch blocks free from the heart of their towers. There was focus. There were grins. Somebody joked and said they should take shots for every tower that fell. Another disagreed, said they should take shots for every block removed.

When it was June and Barrett's turn, he reached, without conferring, and pushed a block free. It fell with a clap on the plastic table. He smiled at June. Unable to read her face, he whispered, "We got this, baby." He nodded and took a long drink. "We got this."

June watched as blocks were removed around the table. Even before the couple ahead of them had removed their block, Barrett used two fingers, one stacked on the other, and pushed a block free. He took a drink and put his arm around June without speaking or looking at her.

June watched a third round, then a fourth, Barrett chipping away at the tower steadily. The towers across the table from her were riddled with holes, and she could see the color of the couples' clothing through them. The tower of one couple already leaned precariously. They inched another block free, everyone watching in silent anticipation, then a light cheer of congratulations when the block fell but the tower remained.

"That was the wrong block," Barrett whispered into June's ear. "They'll never make it now." She looked at him, noting how he studied the others' towers over the rim of his glass as he drank.

It came back around to them and, without a second thought, Barret reached out, but June grabbed his arm.

"What?" he asked.

"I want to do it."

"Equal opportunity," said one of the guests.

"Let her do it," another said. "Show her when in charge women will fuck things up just as much as man. Humans. We're so good at fucking things up."

"What does that have to do with anything?" snapped his partner, who elbowed him in the ribs. "Shut it."

People laughed, and the man shrugged and drank.

June reached her hand out, then paused. She looked at Barrett, who was stone-faced, his eyes glazed with liquor, then followed through. She could feel the pressure as she pressed her finger to the block. It slid slightly, then caught. The pressure grew. Perhaps she'd chosen the wrong one. She looked at Barrett again, who only swallowed. She couldn't stop now, so she put her finger against the block and pushed. She could feel the fibers of the wood sliding against each other, could feel the integrity of the tower absorbing the friction, absorbing the power pushing against the heart of it. June exhaled a long-held breath when the block fell with a click to the table.

"Yeah, baby," Barrett said, kissing her head. "Crushin' it." He shook his glass dramatically to show it was empty. He moved towards the kitchen, where a militia of bottles were lined across the Formica countertop.

June peered around the table at everyone's loose blocks. "Let's reuse these," she mumbled to herself, stacking her loose blocks into a new tower. It came back around to her. She looked to the kitchen, where Barrett's cup sat beside a bottle of Smirnoff. She turned to the tower, choose another block, one that clutched even tighter to the tower than the other as she inched it out. She thought for sure the tower would fall, but when the block slide loose silently into her hand, she placed it on the new tower.

Barrett returned and put his arm around her. "Nice babe," he said, nodding at the new tower. "One thing ends and another begins."

"We'll have two towers by the time we're done," she said, focusing intently on the task before her.

"That's right," he said.

Barrett took the next round and June the following. It was then that towers began to fall. Their collapse was loud, and they cluttered the tabletop. One tower after the other fell but not June and Barrett's. They worked holes into their tower, each skirting the damage of the other, focusing on keeping the whole thing standing.

It was down to just two couples, June and Barrett and a couple they didn't know, but it didn't matter. They saw only their tower with holes and still more blocks that must come loose. How could it sustain even more loss? But it did. They did it together, one block and then another and then another, until the room was silent, all starring at their crooked, seemingly impossible, thing. Then, the crash. The other couple's tower fell. Barrett and June both stood, unaware they'd been crouching, hardly breathing. People clapped and laughed and began talking, stating how much fun they had, telling Marquise and Brianna how great of an idea couple's Jenga had been.

Barrett and June, they just stared down at their tower.

"It defies physics," someone joked behind them.

They took each other's hand. Bing sang "White Christmas."

# Saying Your Name

(for Andrew Field)

## by Kerry Trautman

*Ohio born and raised, Kerry is a founder/admin of ToledoPoet.com and the "Toledo Poetry Museum" page on Facebook, both of which serve to promote Northwest Ohio poetry events. She is a poetry editor for the journal* Red Fez, *and she has served as a judge and workshop leader for the Northwest regional semifinals of Ohio's annual "Poetry Out Loud" competition since 2016. In 2020 her one-act play, "Mass," was selected to be performed as a staged-reading for the Toledo Repertoire Theater's "Toledo Voices" competition. Her work has appeared in dozens of anthologies and journals, and her poetry books are* Things That Come in Boxes *(King Craft Press 2012,)* To Have Hoped *(Finishing Line Press 2015,)* Artifacts *(NightBallet Press 2017,) and* To be Nonchalantly Alive *(Kelsay Books 2020.)*

The first name begins with breath
      through opened throat
    as though beckoning—
        lover to chest,
        child to supper,
        Labrador to the kitchen door.

Tongue semi-closes—
    a faucet's drip into the sink

then a pucker
        forward impulse, urged
                outward like smoke-rings.

The surname sieved by up-front teeth—
        whish-ing breeze through wheat stalks.

Momentary dip of the tongue—
        a pinkie-fingertip into a teacup before
                first sip.

The final timid beat
        like a palm pressing open
                the bedroom door.

# 'Til the Well Runs Dry

## by Steve Cain

I ain't much for city folk. I'm just a country boy from Georgia displaced to Yankee Land, as some of my ex-friends would say. I say ex-friends because there are still some people (more than a few, I might add) that are still fighting the Civil War in their heads and hearts, and they will (and have) excommunicate people from their lives (like myself) because said people have moved out of Dixie. I know it's strange, but it's true. I swear.

We all have misconceptions and biases, I guess. Maybe I'm generalizing. When people hear you're from Georgia, they tend to think you're a dumb redneck, you like country music and NASCAR, chew tobacco, own a bunch of hunting rifles, and say y'all a lot. We do. We chew tobacco 24/7. Women, too. When we come to some place like Cincinnati, we drive around 275 because it's like a racetrack, only we're doing it in our pickup trucks with the gun rack on the back window, blasting Merle Haggard and George Jones cassettes. See, we still have cassette players because we're too dumb to master the technology of a CD player or USB.

By now, you know I'm pulling your leg. That's my problem, sarcasm. We're not all dumb rednecks, just the ones they choose to interview on TV.

When I relocated to Ohio, I settled in a little river village outside of Cincinnati where I was close enough to the big city but far enough away, if you know what I mean. I like people from a distance. I'm not a mean person, not at all, I just like peace, quiet, and no drama.

I was sitting on the riverbank one morning in April, minding my own business, strumming and plucking on my acoustic guitar. If you're from Georgia, it's geetar. It was about eight in the morning, there was a slight fog drifting across the river, and a few ducks floated by, paying me no mind. I was playing a little Hendrix, "All Along the Watchtower." I wasn't playing it left-handed like Jimi because, well, I'm not left-handed. I'm a righty by birth, Southern by the grace of God. Ha! When I finished with Hendrix, I started in on Charlie Daniels, "Long Haired Country Boy." If there's any three songs a country boy with a guitar has to know how to play, it's "Long Haired Country Boy," David Allen Coe's "You Never Even Called Me By My Name," and Johnny Paycheck's "Take This Job and Shove It." If you've never heard them, go get ya some, son!

So, I'm playing, minding my own business, and I feel this presence. I hadn't heard anybody, but I got mad redneck ninja Spidey senses, so I whipped my head around and saw an elderly African American man standing about five feet behind me. I looked him up, and he looked me down.

"Easy, son. I didn't mean to startle you," he said in a voice that reminded me of that Morgan Freeman fella.

"S'alright," I replied.

"You play pretty well," the man said. "Singing's not too great, but the playing's good."

I tittered, not knowing whether to be offended or not. "Thanks, I guess."

"Mind if I sit down?"

"Not at all. Pop a squat. Ground's a little dewy, though."

"When you get to be my age, that don't matter. People expect you to have wet pants."

I laughed again. I liked this guy. I put my geetar pick in my left hand and offered my right to him. "Bo," I said.

"Of course, it is." I knew he was mocking me, but his voice was so pleasant and fatherly that it sounded congenial (see, I know some four-syllable words). He took my hand with his dark, wrinkled hand. "Stone," he added.

"Of course, it is," I joked. We both laughed at that.

"Moses is my birth name, but everybody calls me Stone."

"Why's that?" I asked as he sat down next me.

"Because it's my last name, and I'm more like a stone than a Moses."

"Cold and hard?"

"Old and dark." We both had another laugh.

"Don't mind me," he suggested. "Keep playing."

"What do you like?"

"Know any Otis Redding?"

"Otis? Of course! He's another Georgia boy, like me."

"Yeah, I figured that."

"Why, because of the way I talk?" I asked.

"Well, that, and the fact you're wearing a Georgia Bulldogs hat."

"Yeah, I guess that's a giveaway. You sing?"

"I've been known to, every now and then."

"Try this one." I strummed a G chord, followed by a B7. The tune was unmistakable, a classic, and I saw him smile and close his lips. His tongue flicked out of his mouth and licked his lips. His voice was sweet, youthful, almost angelic, not gravelly as I had expected. His tone was soulful, and it came from a long time ago, from a place far away from where we sat.

"Sittin' in the mornin' sun. I'll be sittin' when the evenin' comes."

I played. Stone sang. It was sad, lonely, and beautiful. When we came to that part, he even did the whistle.

When the last notes ended, I expected Stone to get up and walk on water across the river, into Kentucky and beyond, but he just sat there, lost in thought.

"That was amazing." Stone nodded in reply. "Did you used to perform?"

"Perhaps a bit. A different life ago."

That was all he would say about that, no matter how much I questioned. I finally let it drop. The old man opened his eyes, and I swear I thought I saw them well with tears, but nothing ever flowed from them. He picked up a brown paper bag sitting next to him on the ground, unfolding the opening gently. His fingernails were short and clean. He reached into the bag and took out two lumps wrapped in aluminum foil (in Georgia, we call that tin foil) and offered me one.

I took the lump and asked, "What is it?"

"Biscuit," he replied.

"Thank you." I unwrapped the foil. The biscuit was still warm and smelled wonderful. I took a bite of what I thought was sausage, and I was immediately confused. It *was* sausage, but it had a grainy taste and texture.

Stone looked over at me and smiled. "What's the matter?"

"What is this?"

"Goetta," he replied. "I take it you've never tried it."

"It tastes like sausage and…oatmeal?"

"That's it," he agreed. "What do you think?"

"It's different," I said. "Not bad, but not what I expected."

"I can see that."

"Who woke up one morning and said, 'What'll I have for breakfast this morning? I'm kinda in the mood for oatmeal, but I have a hankerin' for sausage. Oh, I know! Boom, goetta!'"

Stone laughed. It was a hearty laugh, and pieces of biscuit flew out of his mouth. I finished and thanked him.

"You think you'll try it again?"

"I prefer my sausage to be sausage, and my oatmeal to be oatmeal, in a bowl with brown sugar and a few raisins. If you're bringing them around, though, I won't turn 'em down."

Stone closed his eyes and nodded again. "Yep, it's an acquired taste for sure, kind of like Cincinnati chili."

"Oh, yeah, what's up with that?" I asked. "Who puts chocolate and cinnamon in chili? Where I come from, chili is made with beef and beans. We put it in a bowl, not a plate on top of spaghetti! I mean, I've heard of Tex-Mex, but not Tex-Italian! You Midwesterners are a strange bunch!"

"Now, now," Stone scolded. "Don't knock what people like. I'm sure some people think grits are nasty."

"Okay, them's fightin' words," I half-joked.

"And," he continued, "I wouldn't be calling Ohio people Midwesterners. They don't like being called Northerners or Yankees, either."

"What should I call them, then? Northern Southerners? Not Quite Midwesterners? West of Easterners?"

Stone just shrugged. "How about just 'Ohioans?'"

"Yeah, I guess that works." I thought about it as we sat quietly. "Say, you said, 'They.' Where are you from?"

Stone looked off down the river, towards the nuclear power plant. After a minute or two, he said, "A long way away. Been away for a long, long, time, but this has been my home for a while."

I was interested in the man, but I didn't want to press him too much. If he didn't want to share, he didn't want to share. He must have had his reasons.

"Don't like to talk about yourself too much, do you?"

He turned back to me and looked tired. "Why talk about myself? I already know about myself. I'd rather talk about other things and learn more. Besides, the past is the past. Can't go back there, can't go home. Might as well move on. Home is in the heart. I take it wherever I go. Home is here."

It was my turn to nod. Stone put his hand on the ground like he was feeling the earth. He pushed down and started to get up.

"Where ya going, Mr. Stone?"

"Time to go," he answered. As he stood, I saw his pants were indeed wet from the ground.

"Looks like you wet your pants, old-timer."

Stone turned to me one last time, smiling. "Yep, that's what they'll think. Now, play me something off."

"I'll be back down here tomorrow morning," I told him.

Stone nodded and started toward the village. I strummed my six-string again, another Otis Redding ditty called, "You Don't Miss Your Water." I didn't turn around, so I didn't see him, but I could hear Stone's sweet voice on the breeze: "You don't miss your water 'til your well runs dry."

It's been a few months now, and I think about Stone every time I come down to play my geetar. Sometimes I get a feeling like someone is behind me and expect to see him, but there's never anyone there. I don't know if he's alive or if he's still in Ohio. Maybe he found his way back home. Regardless, when I come down here, I always pack two goetta biscuits in a brown paper bag, just in case. There's always one left, but I've got a taste for them now.

# Awaiting Jenny

## by Jessica Weyer Bentley

*Jessica Weyer Bentley is an author and poet. Her first collection of poetry,* Crimson Sunshine, *was published in May of 2020 (AlyBlue Media). Jessica is a contributing writer for several books in the award-winning Grief Diaries Series. She has been anthologized in the 2020 Women of Appalachia,* Women Speak Series Vol. 6, *also in the 2020 edition of the journal* Common Threads, *by the Ohio Poet's Association and in the Highland Park Summer Muse Series* Anthology of Shoes. *Jessica resides in Northwest, Ohio.*

I know you; we are familiar.
A breath on the other side of the door.
It cracked open revealing your handkerchief.
You were holding yellow roses with muck-stained nails.
They trembled from age and longing.
I did not dare go in,
 it was not meant for me.
I ache for my door.
I know your neck at the nape.
Your stubbled chin.
Now simply a slivered portrait as the incandescent light
pours in.
Is she late?
Did she forget the hour?
A woman lost in powder and pearls.

Flitting about trying on her third dress.
She pats her crimson lipstick and adjusts her slip.
You do not falter,
standing still.
A shop mannequin eager to live again.
I peer into your snow globe.
I see your world of glitter.
I hear her now,
grit beneath her hard-soled heels.
A cadence only known by one who has tested time-
and lost.
I recognize the hurried swoosh of her skirt.
Your eyes blaze as if someone struck a match.
She meets your hopeful gaze with hurried breath.
You offer her your jacket as the chill echoes your thrill.
You have come to life.

# Fire Dance
## by Jim Bolone

*Jim Bolone has been a bartender, a drummer, a dockporter, a bouncer, and for the past twenty-five years, a junior high English teacher in Northwest Ohio. Jim grew up in Detroit, Michigan, attended the Detroit Public Schools, and ultimately graduated from Wayne State University with a B.A. in English.*

"Maybe we could model some good things, some marriage-related things," Katie said.

I told her I wasn't sure about any of it and didn't want to devote a portion of my own vacation hosting others' marital problems.

"Would you once and for all just be flexible and hospitable, if not for them, then at least for me?" She raised her brows.

"I can and I will," I said. "But I don't have to like it. This is my vacation too."

"They'll be here in an hour. Please make it good."

Lake Michigan was calm. The waning sun cast a pink glow through the bay window and into the living room. I watched a lone tern nosedive for a meal in a splash before winging back up to a violet-stained sky.

An hour of tranquility ended with the sound of pressed gravel popping beneath car tires.

Katie slammed her book shut and rose. I followed.

A late model Cadillac sat in the driveway. The passenger door opened. Lacey stepped out. She wore visibly tight white capris pants, no panty outline, a yellow tee shirt and judging by the two equally sized points, no bra, and white flip-flops. Her blonde pigtails dangled back and forth. She ran toward Katie and hugged her hello.

"My God look at you! I hardly recognized you Lace!" Katie said.

Lacey placed her hands on her hips. "I know, right? Two and a half years of cardio and a completely new diet and presto, from a sixteen to an eight," she beamed, then looked at me. I faked a smile.

The Cadillac's engine stopped; the driver's door opened. A man grunted and stepped out, looking a little unstable while his thumbs and fingers tapped and scrolled a smartphone. He stopped, stretched his arms, let out a sigh, and then slipped the smartphone into its holster. His green visor revealed a shaved head. He inhaled deep, then exhaled, and placed both palms over the speckled grey stubble of his face. His maroon polo shirt appeared a little small, its armpits darkened with sweat. "Damn," he said. He gazed at us, smiled then approached me. "John Fredrickson," he extended his hand.

Just as my hand met his, I cringed at his grip and returned the favor. "Dang, man, you got a grip," he said smiling while gazing directly into my eyes.

"Travis Bedford," I said.

"Nice little place you got here, Trav." He stretched his handshake fingers, walked back to the Cadillac, pointed his key chain, and activated the back hatch, which slowly buzzed open. He reached in and pulled out a small cooler.

"Beer drinker?" he asked.

"Yeah, but I've got a frig full—"

"Nah, nah, nah," he interrupted. "Not like this shit. Got this stuff in Skokie, Illinois. Small brewery. Nectar, that's what this shit is."

His hands made the rounds to all his pockets, and he appeared defeated.

"Opener?"

"Let me grab one in the house."

"No worries, I'll follow."

I peered through the bay window. Lacey and Katie stood on the beach.

"You sure you don't want to check out the beach first?"

"I'm on vacation, brother. Don't need to hear gals gab. Besides, I see water every day."

"Oh yeah? Where?" I opened the beer bottles.

"Home, man. Grosse Pointe. You didn't know that's where we live?"

"Katie did. Grosse Pointe Park or Grosse Pointe Farms?" I handed him his beer.

"Farms." He took a swig of his beer and swallowed loud. "Are you familiar with the Pointes?" He belched.

"Some."

"Well, my new friend, that's pretty much exactly where we live."

"Small world."

His eyes scanned our place until they stopped at a kitchen window. He walked over, attempted and failed to crank it open. "Stripped. Needs to be replaced."

'Needs to be replaced,' I repeated his words to myself, in disbelief he'd had the audacity to touch what wasn't his. "Thanks," I humored him, and took a swig of my beer, realizing its taste. "Damn, you're right about this," I said.

"I'm always right, especially when it comes to beer. And everything else!" He laughed.

I smiled.

We had a few more beers and during that time I shared a short history of the cottage, including the sacrifices made by my parents to build it. Their trips to furniture stores, cabinet makers, and building supply centers to get exactly what they needed at exactly the right price. John read his beer bottle.

"If I was your dad, I would have sold the place," he said, feeling all his pockets. "Be right back."

The girls returned from their beach walk. Lacey and John settled in, and I helped Katie with dinner—grilled steaks with baked potatoes. After that it was game time. We settled on playing Scrabble. I retrieved the game box and started to set up. We'd agreed on teams, Katie and I against John and Lacey. Katie poured four scotches for the match.

"Hey," she said, "let's make a campfire afterward. It's going to be a clear night and perfect for a fire."

We all agreed. "That sounds relaxing," Lacey said. I nodded and John shrugged, looking at his phone.

As I filled out the score sheets and wrote down John's name he leaned towards me, watching as I wrote. "That's not how you spell my name."

"What do you mean?" I asked.

"It's J-a-h-n," he spelled it out loud. "Not J-o-h-n."

"Really?"

"Yeah.  J-a, not J-o."

I erased what I wrote and changed the O to an A, making a mental note to myself.

"Thanks, man," he said.

"Sorry."

"It's just that names are a big deal, you know? It would be like if I spelled your name T-r-e-v-a-r-." Jahn emphasized the letter "a."

"Yeah, I wouldn't mind," I said.

"I'm sure you would."

"No, I am pretty sure I wouldn't." Frankly, I didn't care if someone got my name wrong. On the list of things important in my life that kind of thing was way down at the bottom. And if I were visiting family or friends. it wouldn't be an issue as much as a selfish disruption. "Ready to play?" I continued.

Jahn smirked. "Question is, are you?"

Katie and I took the first round. This was a good opportunity to prod Lacey about life with my wife as kids.

"So, what were you two like back in the day?" I asked.

Lacey glanced at my wife and smirked. My wife smirked back. "Just a couple of ordinary girls," Lacey said.

"Ordinary?" Katie replied.

"You know what I mean. It's not like we were—"

"Sluts," Jahn interrupted.

"Jahn!  That was totally and completely uncalled for!" Lacey said.

"Sorry babe, but couldn't resist, timing was perfect."

I shot Katie an I-told-you-so look.

She bit her bottom lip for a moment. "We did what typical girls did. We talked about boys, watched soap operas, did homework together. I mean if you're looking for dirt on us there won't be any. Ours was just a basic—but fun—life," Katie said. "Ahem," she continued. "And Jahn, you probably wouldn't have liked us very much back then."

We all laughed. Even Jahn.

Our game lasted around an hour. Jahn and Lacey won.

"Jahn's always been good at spelling," Lacey said.

"Among other things," Jahn said delivering a soft nudge to Lacey's arm with his elbow. Lacey returned the act with a smile and a blush.

I was thinking how the word 'asshole' would have looked in scrabble pieces.

Jahn excused himself and went outside.

A few minutes later, I took matches along with some newspaper out to the fire pit. Jahn was standing, his body silhouetted by a flood lamp behind him on the shed, his face illuminated by his smartphone's screen. The women were inside mixing margaritas.

"So, Trev," Jahn said while staring at his smartphone. "Lace tells me you're in the school business."

"Could say that. I teach. Eighth grade language arts."

"Language arts? Isn't that what we used to call English?"

"Yep," I said, observing his expression change.

"This world is making things really complicated. Funny too."

"How so?"

"English is just one word that says it all. Now there's two." He reached into his shorts pocket, fumbled around a little and pulled out a small pack of cigars. "Want one?"

I declined. He lit up, inhaled then coughed a little. "What about you?" I asked.

"What about me?"

What keeps your fridge full?"

He exhaled. "Drugs man. I mean pharma. Viagra and birth control, some Percocet."

"You must be wealthy."

"Provencal Road and Lakeshore Drive, remember?"

I remembered. Grosse Pointe means you've made it. And if you lived in Grosse Pointe Farms, it's either because you have old money, or you're making a hell of a living. I knew it when I was a kid and went there to dream about what it would be like to live in one of the mansions on Lakeshore Drive. My life felt less when I returned to my house, and part of me hated myself for it, while the other part remained envious.

I gathered some newspaper, rolled it up and began to place it in the pit.

"Let me do that for you," Jahn said.

"No worries. I got it."

"I am a master fire maker."

Certain things in this world remain very personal for each of us. Only we know what those things may be. It could be a process, or a ritual that requires ours and no one else's influence, or unsolicited assistance. Some of these moments offer a zen-like solitude. For me, building a fire had always been one of those things.

He grabbed the newspaper and proceeded to remove pages and ball them up.

"I got this," I said.

"Trev, I'm a master fire maker."

"I bet. But for now, you can chill and let me do the dirty work."

I was being polite. I went back to the newspaper and continued to ball up pages and place them in the pit, while also grabbing key pieces of kindling to work as a starter. Jahn watched. I grabbed some of the larger log fragments and began a first layer, then a second the opposite way, and so on over the kindling, the way I'd done it forever.

"Not going to work, Trev," Jahn said.

"I think it will."

"Too much air."

Coming out of your mouth, I thought. "Nah, it's good. Trust me."

He walked over to me, bent down, and began moving the wood. I nudged his side and he fell over, and while going down he grabbed me and took me with him.

"What the hell, man," I snapped.

He wrapped his arm around my head and squeezed. I jammed my fingers in his side. He let out a grunt and his arm loosened, giving me time to get up and take a good look at him there on the ground. His keys had fallen out of his pocket. A capless pill container lay next to the keys, pills scattered.

"What the hell is that, Jahn?"

He sat up, ran his hands through his graying, thinning hair. He began to shake, which evolved into a sob. I looked up at the house to make sure the girls weren't watching.

He wiped his eyes and shook his head. "I'm sorry."

The back of his shirt was pitted with dirt and gravel, his face flush. I extended my hand. He reached for it.

"You going to be okay?"

"Trying."

"Using?"

He reached for the pills next to his keys on the ground. He threw them into the pit.

I covered them with newspaper. The girls came out with the drinks. They were happy.

"How are you two men doing?" Katie said. "I have tell you, Jahn builds a mean fire," she said, handing us our drinks.

I handed Jahn the matches.

# More than Money

## by Jim Bolone

Before Daylight Savings, I could see yellow lights at the mill.

Pops was there, getting dirty. Later, he'd come home stinking like rotten eggs, and when he smiled, his teeth looked white against the dirt on his face.

Ma was a good mother—strict because she worried about things (most of the time money). When I told her in less than a year I'd be sixteen, old enough to work at the mill with Pa and contribute to the house, she stopped me.

"Over my dead body," she said, tapping her fingertip on my forehead. "You're going to finish high school and do something important."

Things were good when the black blew out of the mill stacks. Saturday mornings we'd all cook up a big breakfast: Pops fried the bacon, Ma made pancakes, while my little sister, Sweet Pea, set the table with me and poured the orange juice. Pea was ten years old. Ma said the first time she saw sweat peas growing in her mother's garden, she knew one day she'd name her daughter them.

When spring came, the stacks at the mill stopped blowing. Pops didn't smell like rotten eggs. I recognized the new smell because I used to deliver coffee for Old Mr. Williams, the owner of the Green Goat Tavern. I carried coffees to places like the beauty salon and the hardware store. I remember the dark inside the tavern, the cool of it from the summer heat, and how the light of the bar showed the colors of the liquor bottles. I remembered the smell of the place.

Pops smelled like the Green Goat.

Him and Ma weren't talking much now. When he was home, he'd tell her he was looking for work. She'd tell him he wasn't looking, and going to the Goat wouldn't find him a job.

Sometimes the phone rang late at night, usually when we were watching TV. Ma would answer, and hang it up after a minute or two and just go to bed.

Pops started coming home late and sleeping in; when he was up, he wanted to be left alone. I wished hard things weren't like this.

After I made toast and oatmeal for Pea, Pops called for me.

"I need you to do somethin'," he said. He smiled, but it didn't look right—it was only in his mouth; his eyes didn't change.

"Okay," I said.

"I need you to come with me. Earn a little money."

Ma came up from the basement. Her and Pops looked at each other, but Ma stared longer and Pops stared at the floor until she went into the kitchen.

"Don't you forget to sweep the basement Henry," she said.

"I will," I said.

"Today," she said.

Pops and I left the house. The past couple of days' worth of rain had seeped into the ground; the damp mixed with the warm of the sun aroused the sense of spring in my nose. Pops drove the truck through town and out a few miles to an old warehouse next to an orchard.

Other cars were there. A crowd gathered behind the warehouse. I didn't know what to think, except maybe we were going to pitch in with others and build something together. Pops parked the truck and turned off the starter. He looked at me and cleared his throat. "You're gonna fight," he said.

I didn't understand those words. "Huh?"

"You're gonna fight another boy." The quiet of the cab made the words too clear, too real.

I looked closer at all the people behind the building—all men. They were forming a circle. "Pops, I can't. I can't do—"

He grabbed my arm; his strong hand squeezed hard. "Now you shut your mouth if you know what's good for ya, you understand?" His eyes had water in them, and the words barely came out from his lips. "I need you Henry, got that? Ma and Pea too. You're gonna come with me, you're gonna whip this boy's ass, and we're gonna get paid for it, understand?"

He put both his arms around me and pulled me close. I didn't want him to let go.

"I do, Pops," I said.

We walked up to the crowd of men, some worked with Pops at the mill; a few boys were also in the mix.

The ground was soft. Pops and a few of the men walked away together. They carried cash in their hands; one of them had a canvas bag. He turned and looked at me for a while. Pops did too.

"Henry," he said. "Come over here."

Then the man with the canvas bag looked over the crowd and said, "Kyle."

A boy worked his way around the crowd and head straight for the man. I did the same for Pops.

"Kyle," the man said, "this here is Henry, the boy you're fightin' today."

Kyle raised his hand to shake. I followed. Our hands gripped; it was a soft shake. A rush of wind pushed through some of the trees in the orchard, and a gang of cowbirds rose like smoke into the sky. Kyle and I watched as they winged overhead.

Pops looked at Kyle, then at me. "You're only goin' three rounds, got it? Whoever wins, wins."

"How do we know who wins?" I said.

"When you can't get up," the man said. "You boys ready?"

"What do we do?" Kyle said.

"Fight."

We walked to the back of the warehouse. The grass under my boots made a sucking sound. Kyle and I stood in the center; his face showed no emotion.

The man with the canvas bag raised his hand. Everyone went quiet. "We got three rounds," he said. "Three minutes per round. The best fighter wins. Boys ready?"

Neither of us spoke. Kyle swallowed hard and looked at me. He raised his hands, clenched them into fists, then settled into a fighting stance. I copied him.

The man with the canvas bag nodded his head at Pops.

"Go," Pops shouted.

The two of us moved around, shuffling side to side, our eyes never breaking contact. Kyle shuffled like he fought before, but his face looked scared.

The men shouted at us to fight. I stared at them. Kyle didn't.

His fist met the top of my forehead. Something inside me told me not to think about anything except what Pops wanted—and the mill. It all sort of became a single thought: beat Kyle.

*All this is the mill's fault,* I thought. *Just win the fight.*

I punched his face and followed through with two more, thinking I'd finished it. Kyle came back in a fury, diving at my legs and knocking me down. I lifted his legs toward his neck. He squeezed my shirt, pulled me forward, and struck my head with both fists.

The man with the canvas bag shouted for Kyle to end it, but Kyle didn't listen; he tried to pull my legs off him, and I threw my fist into his face. I pulled my legs off him. He fell back. Some of the men gasped, others cheered. Soaked and mud-stained, Kyle held his face with both hands.

"Get up goddammit!" the man with the canvas bag shouted. "Come on, get the hell up, boy!"

Kyle held his bloodied nose and stared straight up at the sky.

Pops grabbed hold of my arm and lifted it. "He wins," he said, with the first real smile I'd seen since before the mill closed.

The man handed the canvas bag to Pops and said, "That ain't right."

"Fight's a fight," Pops said. "It's what we agreed."

"Ain't right," the man said, and walked on towards their truck with Kyle trailing him.

I waved my hand and started to say something to Kyle.

"Leave him alone," Pops said.

We were the last ones to leave.


He parked close to the road, away from the house, then reached over, grabbed the canvas bag, and opened it. He pulled out a ten-dollar bill and handed it to me.

"No thanks."

"Whaddya mean, 'no thanks?'"

"Use it for the house, like you said."

He smiled, shook his head. "You did good." He glided the palm of his hand over my hair. "No marks on you either, just a lot of mud."

As soon as we got into the house, Pops put the canvas bag high in the closet and went into the kitchen. I ran upstairs and sat on my bed, shaking a little. My head hurt. I changed my clothes, fast as I could. Pea walked by and saw me and came into my bedroom.

"Where'd you and Pops go?" she said.

"Sommerville. Someone from the mill who lives outside of town a ways."

"You got mud in your hair." Some of the mud had stuck to the ends of it. I pulled on it. "Ma made roast beef for supper, said we're gonna start eatin' different pretty soon."

Pea and I both took our seats at the supper table, but Ma's eyes were on me.

"What the blue blazes happened to your clothes, Henry?" she said.

"Slipped on the front lawn," I said.

Ma stared at Pops. She had an intuition about things, made me feel she knew I just lied. And when she didn't push the issue, it got worse. The guilt made me crazy. She left Pops alone; he ate in a quiet daze.

Ma and Pea did dishes. I went down to the basement to finish sweeping like Ma wanted.

Pops came down too. "You okay?" he said.

"Yeah. Little scared for some reason.

"You did good. You really did, Henry."

I swept some dust into the dust pan and emptied it into the trash. "How many more, Pops?"

He took in a deep breath and looked toward the stairs. "Just a few, maybe."

"I don't like it."

He walked over to me and just stood there. I felt a sort of power over him.

"What about Ma?" I said.

"What about her?"

"Wake up. Henry, wake up," Pops said.
My eyes were half opened. "What?"
"C'mon. We got one this morning."
I yawned and scratched my head, wanting to say something, but I knew better. In minutes, Pops and I were in the truck headin' to Sommerville. He brought the canvas bag from the first fight.
"Do you know who I'm fightin'?" I said.
"Could be anyone. From school, another town. Whoever, you'll beat 'em."
The crowd seemed bigger than last time. Pops handed the empty canvas bag to an old man in overalls; they had a few words. The man pointed his finger at something and disappeared with the bag. Pops motioned for me to follow.
A man, someone I'd seen somewhere before, waited for Pops. The boy next to him turned around.
"This is who you're fighting," Pops said.
David Stenson. He was in my grade, but we hadn't had a class together. His mother died a couple of years earlier.
Pops shook hands with Mr. Stenson. The old man in overalls asked Pops who wanted to hold the money. Pops said Mr. Stenson, who looked around before grabbing the bag.
David and I looked at each other.
"Hey," I said
"Hey."
"Good luck."
"You too."
Some of the men hollered for us to get ready. David walked into the fight area first. The grunts and jeers from

the crowd sounded more like a hogs in a truck than a bunch of men watching a fight.

"C'mon now, throw those fists boys."

For a second, I saw Pops in the crowd. And when he saw me, his face changed and he clapped. I thought about Ma not knowing what I was doing and how Pops asked, "What about her?" I thought about what Pea said about Ma and the suppers and I felt bad. I blamed the mill.

David ran at me and caught me off guard, his fists flailing, one of them catching the corner of my eye. The pain burned through my head. My blood ran hot down my cheek.

"Stop the fight," Pops said. "Stop—"

"No Pops," I snapped. "Not stopping.'" I wiped the blood with my sleeve. David continued flailing. I flailed back, but I didn't see David anymore; I saw the mill. Things went black

Two men held my arms. I saw David's legs on the ground, a couple of men crouched over him. Pops placed his hand on the back of my head.

"Not your fault."

"Got to get him to the doc," Mr. Stenson said.

The crowd had gone. We watched as the old man in overalls helped Mr. Stenson and a few others lift David into the back of a truck. Afterward, he walked over to us with the canvas bag.

"Well, he's back thinking again. Shoot, you knocked the crap out of that kid. Thank the Lord he's awake. Takin' him to see Doc Givens to be safe. Here you go." He handed the bag to Pops, but he didn't say anything.

"What's wrong?" the old man asked. "It's yours. Your boy won, fair and square."

The wind came off from the orchard and spread the stink of decaying apples. Pops moved his hair over with his hand.

The old man looked at me. "You done good, boy," he said.

We went home and he hid the money in the closet. "Go clean up before Ma catches you," he said.

I ran upstairs, washed the dried blood off my face and took a bath. There was a knock at the door. *Ma.*

"Where you and your father been all this time"

"We was just helpin' old Mr. Cotter with some hay bales." She didn't answer.

Pa and the men set up a few more fights, and I won 'em all. He wasn't as excited as before, but *I* was beginning to feel like a regular champ. I had a strategy—the one I invented when I fought David Stenson—which was to look at my opponent not as a kid, but as the mill. It made me into something I wasn't. And I'd win.

One day, after taking Pea to the store for some licorice, we opened the front door and couldn't believe our eyes. Pops and Ma were hugging in the kitchen. Ma had a smile on her face. Pea looked puzzled, but happy.

"Pops got a job," Ma said. "A good one."

"Drivin' truck for a cement company," Pops said. The smile in his eyes and on his mouth were both real this time. "We met at the Goat, and he offered me the job right then and there."

That was it. Pops didn't smell like the Goat anymore. Now, he smelled like cement.

And in the morning, when I saw the shadowed stacks of the mill, I didn't care because there was something in me now. More than the money, I wanted to fight. And I'd be damned if Pops brought home more money than me.

# Lake Michigan

## by Kit McBee

*Kit McBee is a hospitality agent who lives in Ann Arbor, Michigan. His poems have previously appeared in* Of Rust and Glass *and* The Mill *at the University of Toledo, where he studied the humanities. When he's not at work downtown, Kit enjoys going to the gym, practicing martial arts, and singing. Kit would like to thank his friends, family, and the Midwestern art community for their support.*

I woke up
in a ferryboat, I got off
& dashed up hills
of scorching sand in Saugatuck:
sink into Lake Michigan.

There is seaweed around me
in circles, it gobs,
and it falls apart on the surface.
I throw waves
at Emily, face down,
drift to

me, miraculously
unable to swim.

I sit by myself on the beach,
burning, a crowd of people;

it's a landlocked body of water
but I can't see the other side.

# Sheila

## by Kit McBee

Metamora girl picks me up
from the big post office.
An empath on the highway,
she's gonna take the long way.

This small planet runs on chatter:
pinecones
in cup holders on the dashboard.
She steers with her knees.

The song changes:
"Oh, Tommy Fleece—
I don't know what you believe in,
but we've had past lives, and'

(Out the window
yellow leaves and pink leaves
change like slides
on a sensitive microscope)

"He shoulda been mine,
but I was married, I was busy
setting up a website,
'waiting tables at night."

She never turns;
I jump out and think goodbye.
She says, "I'm clairvoyant,
but not when it comes to the economy."

# tonight i broke the sky
## by Joshua Balog

*Joshua Balog (they/them) is a neurodivergent Gen-X garden gnome. They currently reside in Washington, DC, but have roots in Ohio and Tennessee. Joshua spent 20 years in the US Army as a photographer/ videographer and traveled extensively. They love Tom Waits, Lisa Frank, and the Wu Tang Clan.*

the moon is a tiny silver sliver
in a smooth dull greysmeared blue
like the chip in the windshield of an old pickup truck
that patrolled dusty gravel roads that summer
when we both turned sixteen

now i'm reaching up
stretching out my left arm
standing tippy-toed
right arm waving behind to keep balance
i jam my thumbnail
into that tiny crack in the sky
and i push
hard as i can

and just like that day twenty-nine years ago
when you slammed the door
of that old pickup truck
the crack grows legs and runs
creaking and crackling

sounds like trying to get ice cubes out of the tray
branching and splitting to the edges
until it all falls apart

the pieces rain down
skyshard shatterstorm
the whole world is buried alive

and i remember how we had our laps full of glass
pieces in our hair and down our shirts
and you laughed
and now i'm laughing
while i wait to see what crawls out of the glittering
bluegray gravel

i wish you were here

# I Will Unfold Like a Story

by Joshua Balog


I once was a shining elfin child
Long and lean
Unworried and free
Dancing with my dreams
Wings unfurled and glittering

No fool, I
Knew the world was not kind
Sharpened taunts would cut and sting
Painful, but not deep
I learned to twist and weave
And dodge their clumsy words
Queer never sounded like the insult they intended

And I was never alone
I had a merry band of faerie kin
With wheels and noise and grinning defiance
We could see each other's wings
And we learned how to use them
And we all flew away

I left behind honeysuckle, hot tar, and home
For a snowbound settlement of fae folk
Bookish, cheerful and unafraid
Proud to shine and so so glad to have gotten away
From small towns and stagnant crowds
Each winged soul a story unfolding

I will never understand how that winter felt so long
Years of joy compressed just a few months
And shattered in one dark blue night
With bloody death and chaos
From the gun of a small-town demon
In a dark blue hoodie

Ashes fell instead of snow
Grief tied our hearts together tighter
Than promises ever could
I was lost in the skein
Of that fogspun yarn
Til I pulled one end and
Found my way back
Home

Years flowed past like fog
Impenetrable and permanent
Yet vanished in an instant
I struggled to regain myself
But my dreams wouldn't dance anymore
I tried to paint my wings to be
The colors they once were
But they never could hold the hue
So I kept them folded
Until I forgot what they were
No longer an elfin child
Just a sad human covered in ashes

My last chance
To go out into the world
Was submission to conformity
I fit myself into
The shape of a soldier
I squeezed and bent myself

Bits of me tried to break free
Before the ballistic armor was locked down tight
It was not an easy thing
Learning to march rather than glide
Learning to shout rather than sing

Finally, I flew once more
Not under my own power
But by cargo jet and double rotor helo
Over lands beyond the reach of folk's imagination
Some were peaceful, preparing for war
Some were peaceful, recovering from war
And some sad lands bloomed
With orange blasts of rocket-fire
I was made witness in all these lands
And documented their sorrows
With glass lens and electric memory

I returned to my native land
But not to my home
Though I tried to make it so
I was still bound in the shape of a soldier
And covered in ash

Now, after twenty years of binding
I am free of that shape
I will release my wings
If I can find them
I will unfold like a story
And I will dust off my dreams
And ask them to dance

# The Curator

## by Agnes Vojta

*Agnes Vojta grew up in Germany and now lives in Rolla, Missouri where she teaches physics at Missouri S&T and hikes the Ozarks. She is the author of* Porous Land *(Spartan Press, 2019) and* The Eden of Perhaps *(Spartan Press, 2020), and her poems have appeared in a variety of magazines. Her website is agnesvojta.com.*

Deserted, the museum dozes. Artifacts lie forlorn in their glass cases. Their labels peel, curl, the glue consumed by tiny bugs. Helmets and armor, a sword with a broken hilt. Ceramic shards. Beads that once were a necklace. Books in a font only scholars can now decipher. Ancient garments, moth-eaten.

The historic maps in their frames show countries that have descended into obsolescence: borders dissolved, civilizations crumbled like the pressed flowers on the display cards in the natural history section. Stuffed birds sit mounted on branches; the beady eyes lost their sheen and the feathers their colors.

The curator walks from room to room, slowly. The wooden floor creaks under his halting steps. He does not remember when he came here. He unlocks the building each morning, gets out the metal cash box with the tickets and the change. He does not wait for visitors anymore.

The world has forgotten the museum. Perhaps it no longer has need of the past. The curator does. He is on intimate terms with his exhibits. Could answer any question about the countries or the armor. Could name the birds. If anyone were asking.

He is the memory keeper, the sage who could tell you the legends before they sink into the mist of myth. He walks his round and recites the guided tour narrative to himself, the history of the place, so he won't forget.

# The Yew Trees with their Bitter Berries

by Agnes Vojta

The house sleeps
behind curtains of wine leaves.
The black-and-white tiles
lay crooked and cracked
on overgrown paths.

I see, once a year,
my parents' faces
as in a flip book
that makes time visible,
foreshadows endings.

The garden dozes
in the deep dark green
of rhododendrons
and of the yew trees
with their bitter berries.

# Doug Draime Blues
## by Michael D. Grover

*Michael D. Grover is a Florida born poet/writer. His work has been published in print and on the internet, as well as in several chapbooks. In 2020 he published his newest novel* Heavy Metal *on Alien Buddha Press. His newest collection of Poems* Fuck Cancer Poems Version 2.0 *will soon be available. Michael currently resides in Fort Meade, Florida where he lives with cancer and writes haiku.*


Woke up this morning
With those no book blues
Deep down blues
Doug Draime blues
While the do boys do
It keeps me up at night
Worried about salvation
Worried about mortality
That could cut it all short
Worried about the cancer
That keeps me dead most of the time
Just a spectator

Once I spoke with the puppet master
About those Doug Draime blues
He was still out there then
Not much longer
The kind of blues that made him send me e-mails

Yelling at me for not buying his latest book yet
The puppet master smiled and said
*So it's a distribution problem*
Just like this were business
I knew it was his life

Some say the good die young
Fighting all the way down
I say the good grow old
They die silent screaming inside

# daughter godot
## by Nikki Allen

*Nikki Allen is a lover & a writer. She is the author of numerous books, including* Quite Like Yes, Ligaments of Light/Tigering the Shoulders *(Night Ballet Press 2013), and* Hotwire *(River Dog Press, 2021). Her work has appeared in* Gasconade Review, Nailed, Cras*h*, The Pittsburgh Poetry Review, out of nothing, Profane Journal *(Pushcart Prize nominee '14/'15), and* Encyclopedia Destructica *among others. She believes in revolution, strong coffee, the hard knocks & the sweetness.*

Last week I cried because I could not remember your
laugh.
The one that seemed to bring the wind--
a double door blow back
crack belly of wine glass
bring a swivel to every man's neck
in the room.

Gold chain, coffee thigh,
finger snaps to Neutron Dance,
Bloody Mary soldier sweating in fridge
for following morning--
liquor bottle song of your
sweater drawer.
You bought a two seater sports car,

fuck having two kids--
your silk kimono dreams slow drift
in closet among price-tagged sweaters
and lipstick-smashed leather purses,
platoon of stilettos,
orphaned ribbon and pen lid in your wake--
plants and incense headaches,
fishbowl of matches from every bar going south on 75.
Scent of body and illusion like earth herself
crowded in all four hemispheres before shutting door,
bra swinging lazy from its knob.

I am sternum deep in thesaurus
sifting through other words for missing:
*truant, deficient, extinct, gone astray.*
I am a body built around your vacancy.
Would it have been easier
if I looked less like your first love?
Do you know we have the same hands,
that hidden rooms in me reek of you,
that you are a perfume I pray to?
Your name is an underlined hymn.
You turning trend of leaving into art—
your Zeus status mood swings,
what else did I inherit?

When you are the daughter of a myth you learn
which ghost to trust, which god to toss
but you keep them all,
or kill the lot.
Anger is an erroneous word--
maybe longing,
maybe grief.
When I think of you I no longer
envy the men that won you over.

I do not consider the weight of a promise--
brick and feather fall the same.
I no longer drag the lake for clues.
Instead, it is the wedding day I return to.
My father at the altar and you
at the church door, pristine
in a dress the color of bone--
waiting for your father
who never showed.

# Rodney and Rochelle
## by Bobbi Rae

Rodney looked up at me with wet, wide eyes. I couldn't stand the way his swollen lower lip quivered or how his bicycle rim spun lazily, bent at an awkward angle. I couldn't stand the crowd closing in around us, people whispering and pointing their fingers. Most of all, I couldn't stand the heavy heat rising from my chest to my cheeks, like this was all his fault—like I was the victim here. As my vision went all red, I thought back to how this whole mess got started.

I met Rodney early on. When we moved north from Missouri—from emerald bluffs and humid summers, from all the family and friends I'd ever known—I had a hard time accepting lake-effect snow. Here was a place as surreal as Mars to me, and just as cold, too. The worst part? I was the alien.

But public housing wasn't an alien planet; public housing was a jungle.

It was only a few days before school when I first stepped out of the U-Haul. It had a t-rex and the words "America's Moving Adventure" slapped on its side. As it turned out, a handful of days wasn't nearly long enough for me to learn the second hardest lesson I learned that year: urban predators are real, and they disguise themselves in the form of preteen girls with pink-beaded dreadlocks and denim flares.

We were in a neighborhood where kids couldn't possibly exist, so school buses were as scarce as grocery stores. Monday morning came before I even had a chance to unpack my PlayStation and found me confined alone underneath a glass shelter. I picked at scabs on my wrists and read curly-q graffiti that wrapped around the shelter like barbed wire. *"Keep out,"* it said. *"This is our house. You don't belong here."* And it was right: I didn't belong.

Cue Rochelle and the three meanest badgers I'd ever met. They came around the corner of the last apartment building, clad in pink, puffy jackets, Jack Skellington backpacks, and chain-link choker necklaces. By the time I noticed them, it was already too late.

Rochelle is Rodney's older sister. I thought I liked her, for a while, even after her and her friends pummeled me, but those feelings were simple instinct. She had boobs, she wore nice perfume, and she didn't pretend I wasn't there. With Rochelle, I was always the center of attention.

"Hey, dweeb," one of the badgers sneered. "This our stop."

"What you think you're doin'?" Badger number two cracked her knuckles and showed sharp, yellowed canines.

Rochelle raised a fist and they all backed off. "Ain't ever seen you before. What's your name?"

"Er, uhm…" My cheeks flushed red like a muleta. "I…"

"He's nobody, Roach. Just another punk bitch."

She side-eyed her friend, spit onto the pavement at my feet, and smiled. It was a sweet smile, emphasized by tooth and nail, metal bracket and pink bands.

"Is that true?" I shook my head. "If it ain't, then what are you?"

"I'm new," I barely stuttered. "From Missouri."

"Don't care where you from, do we Roach?"

It was her turn to shake her head. Her beads clacked together as her hair whipped back and forth across the fluffy, white liner of her jacket. I caught a whiff of shea butter and coconut seconds before catching a Hello Kitty ring to the jaw.

The flurry of kicks and jabs that followed came from seemingly every direction. I couldn't fight back. They were girls, after all. So, I curled up into a ball, wrapped my arms around my knees, and cried.

When they stopped, I kept my eyes closed for a long time, hoping I'd be somewhere else when I opened them. When the world came back into focus, I was still there, trapped beneath the bus stop bench, with Rochelle's sweet smile inches from my face.

"Mornin', sunshine." The badgers churred behind me. "You were right, though. You ain't a punk bitch. You're less than that, like old gum stuck under the bench."

"And we just chewed yo' ass up," one of the badgers said.

"Oooooh," the other echoed.

Rochelle rolled her eyes. "We did, though. I think I'mma call you Sweet Mint." She gave her friends a round of looks that asked, "What do you think?" and they reaffirmed her status as Queen B.

The worst part? I had a hard-on that was practically bursting out of my Jncos.

Rodney rounded the corner from their building. He shuffled towards the bus stop, gaze fixed at his feet. He was little, smaller even than me, and moved as if it hurt him to do so. We met eyes, he shrugged his shoulders, and looked away as quickly as he could. I swear I saw him shudder.

Rochelle and the badgers dispersed to the far corner of the shelter to piece a cigarette before the bus arrived. Rodney sat right beside me on the bench.

I wiped bloody snot on my sleeve and said, "Hey."

"Hey."

Rodney handed me a watermelon Jolly Rancher. He leaned back on his elbows and cracked his own candy between his teeth. Then, we waited for the bus in comfortable silence.

Over the next few months, we were always together. We never said much; we just existed in each other's company. Me, playing *Legend of Dragoon* for the fifth time. Him, off in the corner with his Game Boy Color. Both of us, riding bikes down College Hill Trail, only slowing for crosswalks and to crane our necks at college girls. Every Monday morning, we met at the bus stop, sure to show up seconds before the bus so Rochelle and the badgers couldn't get their chance to chew either of us up.

We sat together at lunch. We met in between classes to trade Magic cards and peek at a crumpled *Sports Illustrated Swimsuit Edition*, the one with Daniela Pestova on the cover. We laughed in the back of classrooms at jokes that nobody else heard or understood.

When Alec Rogers asked everyone in our homeroom to raise their hand if they hated me, everyone but Rodney put 'em up. Then, Alec kicked my chair out from under me and pushed my trapper keeper off my desk. After the final bell, I waited for the city bus alone with Rochelle and the badgers. They must have smelled blood in the crisp, early winter breeze because they did me in especially good that afternoon.

Rodney had been expelled for breaking five of Alec Rogers' ribs. The news came as a complete shock. How could he have sat back and let Rochelle do all of things she did to me when he had so much fight in him? I felt equally pissed and flattered. No one had ever stood up for me like that before; they usually just laughed or turned the other cheek.

I knocked on his door for the first time that afternoon. It creaked open and a smell like burning plastic and vinegar wafted out. A skinny man wearing loose boxers with sores on his cheeks—Cliff—stood in the doorway. He glared down at me without looking at me. "Fuck you want?"

"Is…is Rodney home?"

He sucked his lower lip and chewed on his cheek as he processed my question. Then, without another word to me, he yelled, "Rodney, somebody here for ya," and disappeared back into the dark apartment.

In the moments before Rodney popped out, I glanced around the empty, yellow-stained front room. It was the same as my living room and kitchen, except the only furniture was a saggy futon and an egg crate piled high with empty bottles and cigarette butts.

Rochelle was sitting on a built-in barstool in the kitchen, rocking gently, holding her knees like I had that first Monday. She was crying. In her black sports bra and gym shorts, I could see bruises running the length of her side. We made eye contact for a split second, and she snapped away in shame.

"Hey," Rodney said.

"Hey."

"Ready to go?"

"Yup."


When somebody broke into our basement storage locker and stole almost everything we owned, including my bike, Rochelle was the one to save the day.

"Here," she said, wheeling me a bike twice my size. With an exaggerated huff, she popped the orange Gary Fischer's kickstand. I gaped up at the bike and gulped. "It's Cliff's, but he won't notice. If he does, I can probably convince him that he hawked it for horse or something."

"Why?" I asked.

She craned her neck, scratching red welts into her skin. Her hip was cocked to the side, and she tapped her opposite foot on the sidewalk. The badgers were sitting around a picnic table watching us expectantly.

Rochelle's voice came so soft I could barely hear her. "Just take the damn bike, Sweet Mint. I know you and my stupid little brother like this kind of crap."

Before I could thank her, she looked back to the badgers, blew them a kiss, and brought the heel of her boot down on my shin. I buckled at the knees, sure she'd broken a bone, but the blow might as well have been a love confession. The girls churred as she stalked back to their picnic table, and I swear Rochelle turned around and winked.

Then, I was back there: slowly stepping away from Rodney's broken body, heart racing. I could only imagine his perspective: an orange streak coming through the pavilion, my maniacal laughter as I cut the handlebars, trying and failing to keep on the sidewalk, the elongated seconds that ticked away as he tried to decide if I was going to hit him or not. Then, finally, the pain of skin tearing on asphalt and bone cracking.

Sirens blared in the distance. I couldn't go to jail. I just couldn't.

I turned and ran without as much as checking on Rodney. Like a coward, I ran home, threw open the door, and bolted it shut, leaving my friend out there alone, bleeding on the sidewalk. Still, I couldn't help but think how awful it was to be me, about how something like that couldn't possibly happen after everything I'd already been through.

Here I was, a stranger in a place where even friends didn't last, and now the only person who wanted to spend any time with me was going to hate me. How could Rodney possibly forgive me? I wouldn't forgive me.

That was the first hardest lesson I learned: no matter how bad things were, they could always get worse.

I'm not sure how much time went by, but eventually there was a knock at the front door. I heard the muffled voices of my mom and someone whose voice was deep with authority. After their conversation, a ringing silence exploded behind my ears. Maybe I fell asleep, I don't know, but when the end of my bed depressed, it was dark in my room.

"What happened?"

I sat up, bleary-eyed, and sniffled. Mom looked tired; too tired to deal with my dumb ass.

"The bike was too big. I lost control."

"Your friend's really hurt, you know?" Fresh tears welled beneath my eyes, but I didn't say anything. I stared blankly at my quilt and picked at its loose threads. "You need to go over there and apologize. His dad agreed not to press charges if you face him like a man."

"Cliff is not their dad," I said, suddenly filled with rage.

Mom rubbed the bridge of her nose and sighed. "I don't really care who he is. You need to go over there and say you're sorry. Right. Now."

Cliff answered the door again. This time, he was dressed in a stained wife-beater and tattered, white-washed jeans. His eyes were as yellow as piss.

I cleared my throat. "I'm here to see Rodney."

He staggered back a half step before catching himself on the doorknob. Then, he leaned forward, squinting. "Oh, you're the fuckwad who bruised him all up, ain't ya? Come to finish what you started?"

"I…" Here they were again, the waterworks, but I couldn't cry. Not in front of Cliff. I took a deep breath through my teeth. "I want to apologize. For what happened."

Swaying, he nodded and motioned me in.

In the kitchen, Rochelle was standing at the stove, stirring a boiling pot. The overhead fan whirred, but that same smell of plastic and vinegar was the loudest thing in the apartment. I realized she was sniffling, and when she finally looked at me, I saw her left eye was black and blue in the shape of Illinois. Her chapped lips curled into a slight smile that I returned without hesitation.

I found Rodney in the bathtub, his eyes closed and his teeth chattering. His torso where I ran him over was red in the shape of tire treads, and his ribs were bruised.

"Hey," he said.

"Hey."

"So, that was pretty messed up."

"I'm sorry, man."

He slid under and bubbles popped on the surface around his head. For a second, I was afraid he wasn't coming back up. When he did, he ran his hands through his hair.

"No worries. Can we go to your place, play some games or something?" I nodded, caught off guard by how quickly he'd forgiven me. "Cool. Lemme get dressed. See you in ten."

Rochelle was once again sitting alone on the singular barstool, face in her hands, shoulders heaving. Cliff was laying on the couch, eyes rolled back, arms splayed at his side with his palms facing the ceiling. I passed between them without saying a word and left the apartment forever.

Rodney never showed up. And, since he wasn't in school anymore and I was too afraid to knock on his door, I never saw him again. Sure, I saw Rochelle and the badgers at the bus stop every morning, but they left me alone for the most part.

I didn't have to endure the awkwardness for long because Mom told me we were moving again. For once, that was okay. Wherever we went next, I knew there would always be Rodneys and Rochelles, but maybe this time I'd find a real friend. Maybe this time things would be different, and the lessons would be a bit easier to learn.

# Five Poems
## by Ryan Quinn Flanagan

*Ryan Quinn Flanagan is a Canadian-born author residing in Elliot Lake, Ontario, Canada with his wife and many bears that rifle through his garbage. His work can be found both in print and online in such places as:* Evergreen Review, The New York Quarterly, Blue Collar Review, In Between Hangovers, Red Fez, *and* The Oklahoma Review.

## First-Team All-stars

It seemed like the unemployment centre
was the place to be.

Everyone was there.

The drunks did not come in
until the afternoon
as mornings are never kind
to a drunk.
The addicts checked the job postings
between scores
knowing full well they would never be hired
as the whores just came in to use the bathrooms.
They already had a good paying job.

The ones that always baffled me
were the ones that came down

in full suit and tie
and demanded an interview
with one of the work placement specialists
who seemed as baffled as I.
What world did they come from?

I could be found at the computers
each day
searching the job bank for something
I knew I would never find.
And I guess everyone else knew it too
because they just left me alone.

I don't know a single sorry person
who was ever hired from that place,
but it didn't stop them all from coming.
Many of us were lined up around the corner
waiting for the joint to open.
With our coffee and cigarettes in hand.

Like a fucking all-star team.

# He's the Weekend

He pulls into a spot by the street
and grabs a cart with a broken wheel
which he pushes back outside.

Like tools being dragged across
the pavement.

It's an older man with a young boy and a girl.
*He's the weekend,*
 I say
sipping at a beer
that will never end.

*Oh right, it's the weekend,*
my wife says.
*I don't see any mother.*

*She's the week,*
I say.

Just then
Louis Armstrong's:
*What a Wonderful World*
comes on.

You couldn't ask
for a more perfect
moment.

# Planning to Steal William Faulkner's Typewriter

We sit out on the patio after dark
listening to the sea come in.

No music tonight,
just the relaxing sound
of the tide.

She finds an advertisement
on her phone
for a treasure hunt in New Orleans
and begins planning a day trip
I have no intention of taking.

*We know our history,* she says.
*Look here, Marie Laveau is the answer
to the first question.  We just have to find her grave
to get the next clue.
It says here that transit is free for
all participants.*

*New Orleans is a bloody swamp,* I say.
*Lets just stay here and listen
to the sea.*

*It would be fun,* she says.

*You're forgetting all the people,*
I counter.
*People are stupid, they are not fun.*

*Look, I found a hotel we can stay at.*
*They have a carousel bar that spins around.*

*Great,* I say.
*How are you supposed to tell how wasted you are*
*if the room has been spinning ever since you sat down?*

She laughs at that one.
*It says here that Tennessee Williams stayed there,*
*you like Tennessee Williams.*

*Not nearly as much as he liked his own sister,*
I mumble.

*Oh, they have William Faulkner's typewriter!*

My ears perk up without me knowing.

*You can't tell me you don't want to see that.*

I take a large swig and finish off my glass of wine.

*What are you thinking?*
she asks.

*I'm thinking that I'm going to New Orleans*
*and I'm planning to steal William Faulkner's typewriter.*

She says she's sure it's behind glass.

*Then, I'll just have to take the damn glass too!*

*So we're going to New Orleans?*
she smiles.

*No*, I say.

*But what about William Faulkner's typewriter?*

I tell her that we need to go in and get a refill.
That old Willie would want our drinks way more than
I could ever want his typewriter anyhow.

The sliding door shuts behind us.
The sea and its long black leather sound
are alone again.

# Grandma Grills

I come back out
after a trip to the bathroom
and find her listening
to Madonna.

*Oh no,* I say.
*We got all this cool music
and I find you out here
with Grandma grills.*

*Grandma grills?*
she questions.

*Yeah,*
*remember that time she went*
*on tv with grills trying to look young,*
*but it was just someone's gyrating*
*grandma with grills?*

I can tell that she remembers
because she changes the song
without a fight.

As though she was trying to slip one in.
I will have to watch her.

The next twenty songs are all classics.
It is going to be a great night.

# Any Man with a Broken Back Could be a Lobster

It comes to the table and I crack its back.
To get at the meat.
My first time.

Any man with a broken back could be a lobster.
That butter sauce ramekin sitting close by.

My wife provides instruction.
She grew up eating lobster.

I pull at the meat
like plunking the strings
of an invisible guitar.

When her dessert comes,
they bring two spoons so we can
pretend we are sharing.

Somewhere in the middle of
the Gulf of Mexico.

I'm in a shirt full of tigers
with matching
socks.

# In Hazel Hollow

## by Jen Mierisch

*Jen Mierisch's dream job is to write* Twilight Zone *episodes, but until then, she's a website administrator by day and a writer of odd stories by night. Jen's work can be found in* Horla, Dark Moments, HAVOK, *and various short story anthologies. Jen can be found haunting her local library just outside Chicago, USA. Read more at www.jenmierisch.com.*

Outside the cabin, the wind howled through the trees, while inside, the old woman's fire was nearly out.

Alma sat still and quiet, wrapped in her patchwork quilt, watching the ebbing flames become embers. In her fingers she held a photograph, barely visible in the dimming space, but she didn't need light to see it. She knew Martin's face by heart.

Rain pounded the roof, poured down the panes. Alma could hear the stream overspilling its banks, surging down the mountainside.

At the foot of the mountain, in room 24 of Rock Ridge Hospital, Nora stood upright. "The baby's breech," she told Joanie. "Mom's eight centimeters dilated. I'm going to need long gloves, ampicillin, and metronidazole. Start an IV immediately." The aide scurried off.

"Did Dr. Georges get here?" Nora asked Lizette.

"Haven't seen him. Must be the storm," the forlorn nurse replied. "And Dr. Reinhardt's still out with the flu."

A thunderclap boomed outside, followed by fluorescent flickers overhead.

"No surgeons," Nora said, squaring her shoulders. "No backup. We're doing this. Get ready."

From the rocky mountain earth, the spirit crept forth. It passed through the rain like a cat through a shadow. It was very old.

Sniffing, it found the soul it sought, and glided forward. It had a collection to make.

Alma smiled, remembering. Martin had been such a clown, making silly faces at the kids until they laughed. His wit and good nature could break through any shyness, any surly mood. He'd been the first to bond, to gain the trust of the children they'd fostered. It took them longer to accept Alma's own cool, steadfast care. But the kids had loved Martin swiftly and fiercely. Especially Nora.

This cabin in Hazel Hollow had been their favorite place on earth; where better to be now? Closing her eyes, Alma heard water splashing and kids laughing as Martin taught them to row the canoe on the pond. She smelled fried river trout, smoke, and marshmallows by the fire pit. She saw Nora's snaggle-tooth grin and felt her hug as she scampered up the porch steps, dirty and delighted after exploring the woods.

*What a funny creature I am*, Alma thought, *a midwife who couldn't have children.* She remembered every baby she'd delivered. Number 366, a girl, had arrived the day before Alma's diagnosis. Then, 366 grams was what the tumor had weighed. The first one.

Outside, the storm shrieked madly, but Alma felt only joy. She would soon see Martin again.

"Cord prolapse," Nora shouted. "And signs of cyanosis. Get those forceps over here! Lizette, prepare the resuscitation equipment."

The laboring mother moaned, a deep, feral sound.

"We're running out of time." Nora exhaled and wiped her forehead with her sleeve. "Need an episiotomy. Joanie, check her chart for lignocaine allergies." Wheels squeaked as the aide maneuvered a metal tray covered with scalpels and syringes.

The old woman shivered, despite herself. Alma was not afraid, but she was growing cold, and the body would do what it would.

Her foster children were grown. They had all walked on, down their different paths. Nora, the bold one, the wild one, only Nora had stayed.

She had never told Nora how proud she was. How pleased she was when Nora chose to study childbirth. How Nora had become a better midwife than Alma had ever been.

She would tell her soon.

The spirit paused at the window, looking in.

The baby, now delivered, was silent.

"Elena, thank goodness you're here. Lizette's got the ventilator. Help her position that mask and check the seal while I stop this bleeding." Turning back to the mother, Nora started stitching.

The blood kept coming. Nora swore. "Joanie. Call the lab for two pints of A negative." The aide sprinted for the phone.

A loud infant wail pierced the tension and burst it.

Nora grinned. Lizette and Elena sagged with relief and hugged one another.

"He's breathing!"

Alma exhaled. Her breath mixed with the fireplace smoke. The two mists curled and twined, embracing like reunited lovers Together they climbed through the chimney into the night sky, and then she was gone.

The spirit slipped away, its work complete, to rest. There would be more duties the next day, and the next.

Before the funeral, Nora stopped by the hospital. The new mother gave her a tired wave. At her breast, the newborn boy drank hungrily. She asked Nora, "What do you think of the name Martin?" She didn't know why that would make her midwife cry.

"I think it's perfect," said Nora, tasting salt as her tears flowed over her smile.

Afterward, Nora drove to the cabin alone. She lit logs in the fireplace and sat at the table. The envelope bore her name, handwritten. She opened it, unfolded the letter, and began to read.